"I want to be part of the investigation."

Mitch should've known this was coming. "You know I can't do that, Kat. You're a civilian now and the closest thing we have to a witness."

"No one needs to know I'm helping."

"I can't let you help, Kat."

"What if you were me?" she asked, her eyes going wide. "What would you want?"

"Wouldn't matter what I wanted, it's what I'd make sure happened."

"Exactly. You'd make sure you were included in the investigation. I'm just trying to do the same thing." She put a hand on his arm and the warmth of her touch melted his resolve.

Having her by his side would be a good thing, right? She wouldn't let her family surround and protect her from this killer, but if she worked with him, he'd be able to keep an eye on her. Problem was he wanted to keep both eyes on her, and not just to be sure she was okay.

Books by Susan Sleeman

Love Inspired Suspense

  High-Stakes Inheritance
  Behind the Badge
  The Christmas Witness
*Double Exposure
*Dead Wrong

*The Justice Agency

SUSAN SLEEMAN

grew up in a small Wisconsin town where she spent her summers reading Nancy Drew and developing a love of mystery and suspense books. Today she channels this enthusiasm into hosting the popular internet website *TheSuspenseZone.com* and writing romantic-suspense and mystery novels.

Much to her husband's chagrin, Susan loves to look at everyday situations and turn them into murder-and-mayhem scenarios for future novels. If you've met Susan, she has probably figured out a plausible way to kill you and get away with it.

Susan currently lives in Florida, but has had the pleasure of living in nine states. Her husband is a church music director and they have two beautiful daughters, a very special son-in-law and an adorable grandson. To learn more about Susan, please visit www.SusanSleeman.com.

DEAD WRONG

Susan Sleeman

Love Inspired

Recycling programs
for this product may
not exist in your area.

LOVE INSPIRED BOOKS

ISBN-13: 978-0-373-44568-4

DEAD WRONG

Copyright © 2012 by Susan Sleeman

All rights reserved. Except for use in any review, the reproduction or utilization of this work in whole or in part in any form by any electronic, mechanical or other means, now known or hereafter invented, including xerography, photocopying and recording, or in any information storage or retrieval system, is forbidden without the written permission of the editorial office, Love Inspired Books, 233 Broadway, New York, NY 10279 U.S.A.

This is a work of fiction. Names, characters, places and incidents are either the product of the author's imagination or are used fictitiously, and any resemblance to actual persons, living or dead, business establishments, events or locales is entirely coincidental.

This edition published by arrangement with Love Inspired Books.

® and TM are trademarks of Love Inspired Books, used under license. Trademarks indicated with ® are registered in the United States Patent and Trademark Office, the Canadian Trade Marks Office and in other countries.

www.LoveInspiredBooks.com

Printed in U.S.A.

Can any one of you by worrying
add a single hour to your life?
—*Matthew* 6:27

Thanks to

My family: my ever patient and understanding
husband, Mark, my daughter Emma
for all the help with editing and Erin
for your graphic design expertise.

My editor, Tina James. Thank you for
continuing to have faith in my writing.

The very generous Ron Norris—retired
police officer with the LaVerne Police Department.
Thank you, Ron, for being there for technical
support on police procedures whenever I need you.
Any errors in or liberties taken with the technical
details Ron so patiently provides are all my doing.

And most importantly, thank you God for not
turning Your back on me when I forget to look to
You first and worry like the characters in this book.

ONE

Something was wrong. Seriously wrong.

Kat Justice flipped the light switch again. Once. Twice. Three times. *Click, click, click.*

Nothing.

She held her breath and listened. No hum from the refrigerator on the other side of the wall, no bubbling of the aquarium. She couldn't even hear the heater that should be running on this unusually cold Oregon day. Just silence, pulsing in the dark.

Someone had cut the power to Nancy's house. Were they still here, hiding in the murky shadows? Should she continue going forward or back out of the house?

A fresh wave of concern sent a shiver down her back.

"Easy, Kat," she whispered as she often had when she'd served on the Portland police force. But calming her nerves wasn't so easy anymore. Not since she'd left the force to work as a private investigator in the family agency. Now she rarely faced danger.

But this new case was different. A man had followed her friend Nancy home. Nancy feared it had to do with her brother Nathan's recent death. She believed he'd been murdered.

Kat had told Nancy to call 911, but the police weren't here. Had Nancy been unable to make the call? After finding the house dark, Kat phoned 911 herself, but she couldn't stand outside and wait for them to rescue Nancy. She had to protect her friend at all costs.

Gun in hand, she slowly set off, putting one foot in front of the other and hugging the dining room wall to make herself less of a target. Her heart thumped wildly as she felt her way to the kitchen doorway.

"Nancy?" she whispered.

No response. She took another step, sliding her foot along the floor. It thudded into something soft yet solid. She knelt down and felt along the floor. A leg. A jean-clad female leg.

Her breath hitched in her lungs as she moved toward the spicy scent of her friend's signature perfume.

"Nancy?" she whispered again, fear ripping open her heart.

She located her friend's neck and checked her pulse.

None.

For a moment she could only sit in horror. Nancy was dead. Her old college friend, the woman she'd just reconnected with after seven years, was gone. Kat had failed her.

No, God, no. Not this. Not Nancy.

A sound drifted through the darkness. The barest of sounds like a whisper. Kat held her breath and listened. Soft footfalls. One then another, moving on carpet in the next room. Step after slow step. Heading her way.

He's still here.

Hands trembling, she jerked back against the wall.

Think, Kat. Think.

She couldn't help Nancy now. She needed to retreat to safety and then apprehend the killer if she could do so safely.

She searched the shadows, straining her eyes. Darkness and more darkness, split only with a slice of light from the open doorway. She heard the sound again. Slow yet stealthy. He was closer now. She had to move. If she sat here, she'd die.

She stayed low, crossed the room and followed the wall

retracing her steps toward the door. She glanced around the corner.

A hulking male stood in a shadow cast from a streetlight. Dressed all in black with a ski mask covering his face, he closed the door behind his back, plunging them into complete darkness.

"So glad you could join our little party." His voice was low and gravelly, yet oddly excited.

Her mouth went dry, and her throat tightened, cutting off her air. She had to get out of there.

The back door.

She rose and backed away, tripping over Nancy. Her arms flailed in the air, searching for anything to break her fall. Her fingernails scratched down a wall, but she couldn't grab hold. She landed with an *oomph* next to her friend. Her gun slipped out of her hand and skittered across the wood floor.

She turned over. The moon broke free of heavy cloud cover. Silvery light filtered through the window making her assailant look otherworldly. Large, muscular, he took slow measured steps as if he had all the time in the world.

Father, please. Don't let me die. The prayer filled her mind, but panic dragged it away in a flash.

Rolling over, she scrambled toward the kitchen.

His heavy footsteps followed, faster now. *Clunk, clunk, clunk.* Swift and sure. She felt him near her. Heard him breathing, raspy and harsh.

She risked a peek behind. He was close, standing over her. She gave one more lunge into the kitchen, the back door only a few feet away now. She clasped the cool doorknob, but a hand shot out and grabbed her by the ponytail, jerking her head back and dragging her toward Nancy.

"No!" she yelled and kicked, hair ripping from her head.

He slammed a knee in her back, forcing her facedown onto the ice-cold tile. Air rushed from her lungs and she struggled to gain a breath as he caught both of her hands behind her back.

"No," she wheezed out and freed a hand. She grabbed for anything she could touch, connecting with latex gloves, then reaching higher and clawing with her fingernails. Digging deep and hard.

He swore and yanked her hand away, wrenching her arm and pinning it next to the other one. She bucked, but he was too strong. He bound her wrists. The slash of thick tape pulling from a roll the only sound besides the thudding of her heart echoing in her ears.

Please, God! Please don't let this happen!

Hard fingers dug into her arms as he flipped her to her side then straddled her hips, holding her in place with iron muscles. "You'll pay for that scratch, Kat."

How did he know her name?

"Do I know you?" she asked, though she was certain she'd never heard his voice before.

"Nancy told me all about you and your little part in this. So glad I can clean up all of her messes in one night."

He thought she'd discovered something about Nathan's death, and he was going to kill her before she could act on it.

"I don't know anything," she said, filling her tone with as much conviction as she could, but it came out breathless and wispy.

"You think I believe that?"

"It's the truth."

He bent low. Got in her face and laughed. Rumbling. Horrible. Sadistic. His breath was stale with cigarette smoke and mixed with cloying aftershave. For some reason, that made it all abruptly real, and she realized she was about to die.

Terror took hold. Terror beyond her wildest imagination. Her heart threatened to burst from her chest.

"No." She bucked harder, upsetting him for a moment.

He had to grab the wall to steady himself. "Just like your friend. Fighting when you have no chance."

He drew back and sent his fist barreling into her face. She felt her nose give. Blood poured freely down her cheek and into her mouth, tasting metallic and thick. He laughed as he wedged a small flashlight under his arm then pulled an elastic cord from his jacket.

"Nancy had no business talking with a private investigator. Your death is on her hands, not mine." He aimed the light at her arm and secured the cord just above her elbow.

He pulled something else from his pocket and held it up. The beam from his flashlight shone through it.

A syringe!

A sob rose in her throat, wild and desperate.

"This is more fun that I thought it'd be," he said, thumping the vein at the bend of her elbow. "Don't worry. You won't feel a thing. You'll just slip off to Never Never Land."

She looked up at his blistering, angry eyes, and prayed. Prayed for Nancy, dear sweet Nancy, but mostly, mostly she prayed he wouldn't succeed in killing her, too.

Detective Mitch Elliot searched the hazy street of the older Portland neighborhood for the correct address. This was not what he wanted to do tonight. Not after a day of dead ends in his latest homicide investigation. He should be home tossing a thick steak on his new gas grill. He could already taste the tenderness of the aged beef that he'd enjoy while listening to cheers of the Trailblazers game. A perfect way to improve a hideous day.

Yet here he was. Chasing down Kat Justice's wild voice mail.

She didn't even want him here. She'd called his partner, Tommy. But Tommy had an appointment and they were expecting a call on a case. So he'd forwarded his phone to Mitch.

Now he had no way to reach Tommy and it was up to him to check out Kat's claim that her friend was in danger.

He located the house and killed his lights. No sense in alerting anyone to his presence. He pulled to the curb several houses down and got out to assess the situation. An SUV sat in the driveway. Kat's? Maybe. Or it could belong to the homeowner. Kat had said the front door was open when she'd arrived, but now it was closed and the house was dark. It had taken him ten minutes to get here so maybe she'd already come and gone.

Easing closer, he listened. Nothing but crickets chirping from the postage stamp of a yard. He couldn't go rogue and bust in. He wasn't a private investigator working for the family agency like Kat, but a sworn officer with protocols to follow.

He pulled out his phone and scrolled to Kat's number. Dialing, he listened at a window. The phone chimed from inside the house.

She was here. It kept ringing.

C'mon, Kat. Pick up.

No answer. Rolling to voice mail. He dialed again. Same response.

Shoot. This was *not* how he'd planned to spend his night off. He lifted his gun and turned the doorknob. Unlocked. Not good.

"Help!" He heard a woman's voice. Maybe Kat's but it was so high and desperate he wasn't sure. It was enough, though. A cry of distress gave him the right to enter.

He burst inside. "Police."

The sound of a scuffle to the left took him in that direction. Gun outstretched with flashlight underneath, he turned the corner and directed the beam ahead. A masked man bolted out of the room. Kat shifted on the floor, her arms bound behind her back. Her nose was swollen and bleeding and a woman's lifeless body lay nearby.

Mitch wanted to rush ahead and check her out, but he stayed in defensive mode and eased slowly forward, noting a syringe on the floor. "Are you okay, Kat?"

"I'm fine," she said between deep breaths. "Go after him."

"You're sure?"

"Yes. He killed Nancy. Don't let him get away with it. Go!"

He didn't wait for more encouragement but leaped over both of them and charged out the back door. Adrenaline flowing, he cautiously moved to the corner of the house and saw the killer jumping into an older model van. Revving the powerful engine, he raced away.

As Mitch ran for his car, he caught a glimpse of the license plate too coated in mud to identify. Still, he noted it was a white, full-size van with a large black circle painted on the hood with red printing. Some sort of logo, but the rain and fog obscured a clear view of the words.

Hitting his lights and siren, he squealed onto the road. He radioed in his pursuit, reported the murder, then turned his full attention to avoiding an accident. They flew down tree-lined streets, houses blurring by until they careened onto a main thoroughfare, narrowly avoiding a collision. Soon the wail of other sirens on the way to help mixed with his. Good. The more officers coming to the party the less likely their suspect would get away.

They headed toward a train crossing with red lights already flashing and a thick wooden gate lowering.

"Gotcha," Mitch said as he mentally prepared to apprehend the killer.

But the van sped up and crashed through the gate, sending debris flying. He whooshed across the track inches ahead of a train.

Mitch slammed on his brakes, his car fishtailing to a stop

seconds before the rumbling train thundered across the tracks. Slamming his fist on the wheel, he radioed the killer's location. He was out of the chase now. When the train cleared, the killer would be long gone. Mitch could only hope one of the officers on the other side of the tracks would catch him.

Adrenaline ebbing, he backed up and retraced his route to the house at a more sedate speed. No need to race back and risk an accident. He'd been gone long enough for paramedics and patrol officers to have freed Kat from the restraints and tended to her injuries. Now he'd have to take her statement.

If she was willing to talk to him—and that was a big *if.*

Seven years had passed since she'd declared her rookie crush on him. Though he'd tried to let her down easy by telling her about his policy not to date coworkers, she hadn't taken the rejection well. Well, hah! She'd taken it badly. Very badly. They'd been able to work in the same department, but man, it was tense every time they'd run into each other before she left the force.

Not knowing what to expect from her, he turned onto the street and spotted Tommy's car parked near two cruisers and an ambulance, their lights swirling into the fog. Good, this was better than Mitch had hoped. Tommy would take Kat's statement while Mitch worked the other aspects of the investigation.

Tommy jogged down the front steps as Mitch parked.

"Glad to see you're here already," he said, climbing from his car. "How'd you hear about it?"

"I'd barely gotten out of my appointment and stopped my phone from forwarding when a uniform called to tell me what had happened." Tommy looked at Mitch's empty backseat. "I see you didn't apprehend the suspect."

"A train got in my way, but uniforms are still in pursuit."

Tommy mumbled something under his breath and tipped his head at Kat who sat on the front porch with a medic ministering to her. "Kat's friend didn't make it, and she's really freaked out."

"Any idea what's going on here?"

"It has to do with a case she's working on, but I couldn't get the details out of her."

Odd. Tommy could make even the most noncompliant suspect confess, so why couldn't he get the woman who'd sat next to him in a patrol car for five years to tell him what was happening? Maybe Kat had completely collapsed—although that would be another oddity, as she was one of the strongest women he'd ever met.

"She too upset to talk?"

"Nah, it's me. I kinda blew up at her." No surprise, there. Tommy's Irish temper often got in the way. "When I saw what the creep did to her, I lectured her about going in without backup."

"You didn't."

"I know. I know." He held up his hands. "We both would've done the same thing, and I had no business yelling at her." They were taught to protect life at all costs and sometimes that meant risking your own. "But man, he could've killed her. And I—" He shrugged.

"You lost it."

"Yeah, and now she's upset with me on top of everything else. So can you talk to her? You know, help her deal?"

Not at all what Mitch expected him to say, not with his history with Kat.

"Can't you call her family to help?"

"Trust me. The last thing Kat would want is for me to call them. She's too independent for that."

Mitch knew Tommy was right, but that still didn't make Mitch the best one to help. "You know I'm not the right choice for this."

Tommy raised a brow. "What? You talking about the way

you brushed her off? That was a long time ago. I'm not sure she even remembers it."

Mitch wasn't as certain. When the medic headed for her rig, he looked at Kat, hoping to judge her mood.

Sitting with her legs pulled up tight in the circle of her arms and her head resting on her knees, she met his gaze. Anguish flowed from her expressive eyes. Her nose had stopped bleeding but was already swelling. Probably broken.

"Look at her, man," Tommy said as she lifted an ice pack to her face. "How can you say no?"

She shivered and stared into the night, her eyes vacant and full of pain. Mitch hadn't seen her for two years, maybe longer. Not since her adoptive parents' funeral. They were murdered in a robbery gone wrong. Her adoptive father was a former police officer so all the rank and file had shown up to pay their respects.

He'd watched her that day, unable to take his eyes off her as she stood in her dress blues for the very last time in her career. Perfect posture keeping her back stiff, shoulders high, arms at her side. Looking strong and in control. Until he caught sight of the raw pain in her eyes and his heart turned over and broke for her.

But now? Now he didn't know what he was feeling and that scared him more than he'd like to admit. But he just couldn't walk away.

"Fine. I'll do it," he said. "But I'm not to blame if it upsets her even more."

"Just handle her with kid gloves and you'll be fine."

Mitch headed for the house. Kid gloves, right. How was he supposed to do that when each step gave him a better look at how this creep had beaten her up, making him madder than he'd been in years?

He fisted his hand. He had to keep things professional. Do

his job. Encourage her to recount her horrifying experience. Then help her deal and do everything within his power to catch the killer before he came back to finish the job.

TWO

Kat couldn't get her heart rate to slow, and the thunderous look on Mitch Elliot's face as he strode up the walk didn't do anything to help. She should look away from the man who'd once rejected her, but she couldn't take her eyes off him.

Over six feet, and dark, he looked dangerous coming out of the mist. Not dangerous like the suspect, but dangerous like a man who refused to be ignored. He always managed to get to her in a way that tested her decision to steer clear of relationships.

The wind gusted, ballooning out his jacket and blowing tiny needles of rain in her face. She shivered, a tremor starting at her neck and working down her body.

Mitch stopped in front of her and, without a word, he shrugged out of his windbreaker and handed it to her. As the jacket dangled from his finger, she thought to refuse it, but another shiver had her sliding her arms into the sleeves and feeling the gray flannel lining laced with his musky scent resting soft against her neck.

He took a deep breath and squatted in front of her. Closer than she'd like, he didn't make eye contact. Instead, he stared beyond her—maybe at the door or at the officer standing watch. He needed a shave and in this hazy light, he looked more like a bad boy than a homicide detective.

"You give anyone your statement?" he finally asked, still not looking at her.

"Not formally." She looked at her hands, remembering how she'd clawed the killer. "I scratched the suspect and the tech scraped my nails for evidence, but otherwise Tommy's kept me out here."

Despite the warmth of his jacket and the scent of his cologne clinging to the fabric, she shuddered again, and that seemed to bring his assessing, steel-blue eyes her way. "You're in shock, Kat."

"Huh?"

"Shock. That's why you're shivering."

"I'm fine. I just need a moment." Intending to talk with Tommy—maybe escape the piercing eyes that seemed to cut to her core—she rose. Her vision blurred on the edges, and she swayed.

Mitch shot up and clamped his hand around her elbow. "Easy, Kat."

She shook it off and used the column for support, but waves of dizziness continued to assault her. She never fainted. Never. Not at gory accident scenes. Not at homicides. So why now? Why here in front of all these law enforcement professionals?

She didn't want to seem like a rookie, falling down at the sight of a body, so she sat down, before dropping into Mitch's arms embarrassed her more. She lowered her head between her knees and gulped air.

She felt him sit next to her, the warmth of his leg settling into her chilled skin. He took a deep breath before exhaling loudly, and she wanted to turn to him and let him hold her. To make this all go away for just a moment in the circle of his arms. But she wouldn't turn to the man she'd once had a huge crush on.

A rookie crush like all the female recruits wanting him for their training officer.

Never happened. Not for her or for the other women. The captain must have seen them all swooning over those amazing blue eyes and only assigned male recruits to Mitch.

Her crush ended, but not before she'd let him know of her interest, and he'd firmly rejected her. Now here he was, sitting next to her, and she needed to start acting like the professional she was and not some woman he cast aside—or worse, a victim.

Father, I know what I'm going through is nothing compared to the loss of Nancy, but please help me get through this. Help me stay strong, do what I'm trained to do and find her killer.

She lifted her head and waited for the world to right itself.

"Better?" He watched her with his trademark stare. One eye narrowed, his mouth lifting a bit on the same side, the other eye dark and deadly intense.

She nodded.

"Good. How about telling me what happened?" He pulled a small notebook from his pocket, his gaze saying this was all business for him.

All business…and the fact that it bothered her made her even more upset. "Nancy called me. She's an old friend from college and a client of our agency."

"And Nancy's the deceased?"

She flinched at the clinical terminology. "Yes. Nancy Bodig."

He jotted her name on his pad. "Go on."

"Her twin brother, Nathan, died two months ago when his car plunged into a ravine. It was deemed an accident, and she didn't question the ruling until last week."

"What made her change her mind?"

"She kept Nathan's cell phone active so she could call his

voice mail. You know, just to hear his voice every now and then. But the last time she called, a man answered."

Mitch's eyebrow rose. "And she thinks this means his death wasn't accidental?"

"Sort of," Kat answered, knowing how lame it sounded. "He never went anywhere without his phone but the investigating officers didn't find it at the accident scene."

"That doesn't mean he was murdered. The phone could've been stolen or misplaced. Even lost in the crash area. Then someone found it and decided to use it." He sounded so detached—professional like a cop should be.

Now she knew how it felt to be on the other side. To be a victim. All she wanted to do was mourn the loss of a friend. Instead, she had to recount how she'd failed Nancy. It was almost too hard to go on. But if she didn't, this killer would never be caught.

She took a deep breath. "The state police said the same thing when Nancy approached them. I even told her that when she first came to see me."

"But?" He waited, pen poised over his notebook.

"But then she told me she checked his online phone records. There were no outgoing calls and there was only that one incoming call after his death. Since then, I've monitored the account. Nothing."

"Maybe the phone company made some sort of mistake routing that call."

"I checked into that, too. Trust me, I checked everything I could about that phone. It all points to someone possessing Nathan's phone. But not for regular use. So why keep it? Why answer only on that one day?"

"Good questions, I suppose."

"That's why I took her case and agreed to find out who had it." She shook her head. The truth of her failure was about to come to light, and she waited until she'd stemmed off another round of tears. "I didn't think she was right about the murder, but after tonight—" Her voice broke, and she couldn't finish her thought, but simply stared down at the mossy sidewalk in front of her. The sidewalk she'd run up not an hour ago and found Nancy's lifeless body.

She felt as if she might lose it. Really lose it like she did the night her birth father killed her mother right in front of her. She was only eleven. A child. Watching the man who'd beat her mother time after time, finally going too far. Her mother, after years of letting a man control her every move, lying there. Lifeless.

The pain swamped her as another wave of grief rose up over her adopted parents who were gunned down in a robbery just a few years ago. Another senseless loss and a reminder of all the horrible things that had happened in her life before they'd rescued her.

"You're certain tonight is related to the brother's death?" Mitch asked, his gentle tone pulling her head back up. His eyes were soft and warm. He understood the pain of what he was asking her to do and he was urging her to go on.

She let his warmth chase away the horrible sights and smells of violence and focused straight ahead. "The killer said Nancy shouldn't have involved a private investigator in this and that it was her fault he had to kill me. He knew my name and it sounded almost like he had Nancy lure me here to kill me, too."

"Back up." His voice turned sharp. "You didn't say anything about luring you."

"Like I said in my message, Nancy called and said a guy followed her home. She thought it had to do with Nathan's death. When I got here, she was already dead and the creep was waiting for me. He told me it was good that he could clean up both of Nancy's messes at one time."

He winced as if the memory of finding her didn't sit well

with him. "So you think our suspect forced her to call you so you'd come over?"

"Maybe… It sounds farfetched when you say it, but after what happened here, I honestly don't know." She drew in a deep breath before going on. "Also Nancy was supposed to call 911. So why didn't she?"

"Maybe he overpowered her before she could dial."

"Or she didn't make the call because he was standing next to her forcing her to call me."

"At this stage in the investigation, anything's possible," he answered just like a good cop would. They were taught to look beyond the obvious. Not form an opinion early on or it might cloud their judgment. And never, never rush to a conclusion.

"So how about the suspect?" he asked. "I got a good look at his build and saw he wore a mask. Is there anything you can add to help ID him?"

She thought about it. About him. About anything that could help, but even though it seemed to go on forever as he'd held her on the floor his angry eyes seething at her, now it flashed by in a blurred memory, and she couldn't come up with much.

"Nothing, other than he was strong," she said. "Crazy strong. He tried to inject me, and it took everything I had to fight him off until you got here." She looked at her wrists, red and irritated from the tape, and could still feel the creep binding her hands and pressing her face into the cold floor. "He thinks I know something about Nathan's death. Except I don't have a clue why Nathan *or* Nancy were killed." She forced nonchalance into her tone that she didn't feel even as a swift shiver confirmed her fear.

Mitch leaned over and tugged the jacket closed but didn't let go and looked deep into her eyes. "We need to get you out of here."

"I want to stay to make sure Nancy's treated right." She took a deep breath and forced away more tears.

"We're all professionals here, Kat. She'll be handled with dignity." He let go of the jacket and stood, offering a hand on the way up.

He was right. Nancy didn't need her now. She'd needed her earlier. Before a man murdered her and Kat failed her.

She took Mitch's hand and swayed again. He put his other hand under her elbow. She wanted to shake it off and be strong—be like the police officer she used to be where nothing made her feel so lost and dead inside. But she couldn't find the resolve to do so and wasn't sure she ever would again.

Mitch pushed open the front door to Kat's town house and stood back to let her enter. She slipped past him, went to the kitchen adjoining a two-story family room with soaring windows and dropped her keys on the laminate counter.

He shouldn't be here. Not in her home with her personal things all around, making him think of her as a person and not a victim in one of his cases. His first instinct had been to have a patrol officer take her home, but he'd told Tommy he'd try to help her cope. Plus he wanted to check out her house to make sure their suspect hadn't decided to come here to finish what he'd started.

And maybe, if he stopped to admit it, something in his gut said she needed him. Not some unknown officer, but him. Mitch Elliot.

He hadn't felt needed in years. Avoided it, actually, ever since his partner, Lori, was gunned down in front of him. Sure, he took a bullet himself that day, but he'd lived. She hadn't.

He felt the scar on his neck, the raised reminder of how fast someone he loved could be taken from him and why he was better off going it alone in life. No matter how good it felt to discover he could connect again with a woman like Kat, he'd never risk another loss.

She turned and big, haunted eyes stared at him. His gut squeezed like a vise, but his fingers still resting on the scar kept his mind on business.

"Thanks for bringing me home," she said. "And I haven't thanked you for your help at Nancy's house. If you hadn't come along—" Another violent shudder wracked her body.

"You're welcome." He felt as if he should say more but opted not to dwell on what could've been.

He closed the door and took in the apartment's white walls and dull beige carpet. Moving boxes lined the far wall and minimal furniture filled the small living space. Fire had destroyed her house last year when a drug dealer tried to burn out the woman she was protecting. This place was so not Kat. Her walls would radiate color. Bright, bold color.

"So when will your house be done?" he asked, wiping his feet on the small mat by the door.

"How do you know about my house?" She bit her lip, but her gaze never waivered.

"Tommy's my partner, remember?"

"Right." She frowned and tugged the jacket tighter.

But a tug of a jacket wouldn't keep him out of her business. Partners shared a lot—were like old married couples in so many ways—and he knew all about Kat's life. More than she'd likely want the man who'd once rejected her to know.

The sooner he did his check and got out of there, the better for both of them. "I'll do a quick walk-through of the house then take off so you can rest."

"You think he came here?" Her voice rose in alarm.

"Nah," he said, to calm the renewed fear sparking in her eyes. "But it'd be a good idea to make sure. You stay here."

He didn't wait for her agreement but went down the hall. He checked each room, each window, to be sure the locks were secured and the blinds closed. As he headed back to the family room, his cell rang, making him jump.

"What's up, Tommy?" he answered, passing by the kitchen and seeing Kat making coffee.

"Suspect got away."

Mitch huffed out a disgusted breath and started up the stairs. "What happened?"

"Does it really matter? He's gone."

"Then it's up to us to bring him in." Mitch tried to sound optimistic but until he knew if the scene provided any strong leads, he couldn't really be so sure they'd catch him.

"You get Kat home all right?"

"Yeah." He glanced at her one more time before making the turn on the landing.

"She doing okay?"

"Not really. I'm clearing the house right now, but when I finish, I'll insist she call someone to spend the night with her. Maybe her sister or one of her brothers."

Thanks to Tommy's nonstop chatter, Mitch knew all about the Justice family. Kat had three brothers and one sister. All of them were adopted. And all of them were former law enforcement officers who gave up their careers to find their adoptive parents' killer. Now they continued to work together in a private investigation agency. No one better to care for her than her siblings.

Keep telling yourself that and maybe you can go home without a backward glance.

"Kat will never go for it," Tommy said.

"I thought you said they were all tight."

"They are, but if this guy is really trying to kill Kat, she won't want them mixed up in this."

"I don't follow." He checked a bedroom with a small bed and more boxes piled to the ceiling.

"She's a worrier. She's seen too many people she loves die and lets it get to her. So if there's any chance they'll get hurt, she'll keep them out of it. She doesn't even date. As she says, why find someone just to lose them."

Mitch understood that. How he understood it. Losing his parents and Lori, plus his sister Angie's plunge into the black hole of drugs, guaranteed that. Still, it didn't fit the woman he thought he knew. "I never figured her for a worrier."

Tommy laughed. "She puts on a tough front, but when it comes to people she loves, she's a bowl of jelly."

"Good to know. Still, I'll have to insist she call them." He went on to the next bedroom. This one was obviously Kat's— neat, orderly and box free.

"Of course you will. Just wanted you to be prepared when she balks at it."

Mitch opened the closet door. "You about done at the scene?"

"Yeah. I'm heading back to the office to get a jump start on this if you want to come in." Not a request. More of a plea to help find the person who'd manhandled and almost killed his former partner.

"Want me to bring a pizza?"

"Yeah, man. That'd be good."

"I'm putting mushrooms on it, so deal." As he disconnected, he heard Tommy laugh over their longstanding debate about where fungus belonged. According to Tommy, it wasn't on a pizza.

Mitch cleared the small bathroom, checking behind the shower curtain, then went to the stairs where the nutty aroma of fresh coffee drifted up.

Kat was standing at the bottom. She still wore his jacket and held a steaming mug. "I made coffee. You want a cup?"

Not really, but with the way she looked up at him all wounded and sad as if she needed him, he couldn't say no. "Sure."

She went to the kitchen, and he considered how he was

going to convince her to let a family member spend the night. She had a reputation for being stubborn and headstrong. Not something he had much experience in dealing with when it came to women.

"I'm assuming we're clear," she said, joining him with a second cup.

"Yes." He took the mug and put some distance between them. He waited for her to say she could've done that herself, but she just gave a sad, halfhearted nod. Not a good sign.

"You shouldn't be alone tonight, Kat." He took a sip of coffee and nearly groaned at the strong, freshly ground taste he loved.

"I'm fine." Her shoulders went up a notch.

He regarded her for a moment and she held her rigid posture under his scrutiny. She was trying so hard to keep it together, but he saw the crack in her strong veneer ready to crumble with the least little blow. "I'm not sure you're a good judge of how you're doing right now."

She raised a brow as if daring him to protest. "I appreciate your concern, really I do, but there's no need to bother anyone else." She gave him a tough-as-nails look, then walked into the family room almost aimlessly as if she had no idea what to do with herself. She paused staring ahead. Then, as if reaching a decision, she put her mug on a table and dropped onto the sofa.

He followed and decided to take a firmer stance as he sat next to her. "I'm going to call one of your brothers or your sister."

"No! It's late and they don't need to get involved in this mess."

"Truth time, Kat. What's going on here?" he asked, expecting her to reinforce Tommy's take on things, but hoping if she did, he'd find a hole in her logic.

"It's nothing, it's just—" She looked down and started frantically rubbing her wrists where the skin was angry and raw. "This is the first case I've headed up at the agency. Ethan and Cole have pretty much been in charge. Makes sense, I guess. They're the oldest and have the most experience. But still, I begged for a case. Told them I was ready. Now I screwed up and…" Her voice faded away.

Not the answer Tommy had prepared him for. "And you don't want them to know about it."

"Yeah." She kept picking at her wrist.

His mind flashed back to the moment he found her. Bound and helpless, a terrified glaze to her eyes. These very wrists strapped behind her. She seemed now as if she could hardly bear the memory. He took her hands, stopping her from damaging the skin even more. He held her icy fingers as he waited for her to look up at him. When she did, he smiled to help ease her anxiety, but she stared at him looking lost so he plunged ahead. "Your family will hear about this on the news by morning. Maybe you should tell them before that happens."

"I just can't handle facing them tonight. Tomorrow, but not tonight."

He could feel the tension radiating off her. He wanted to do more than hold her hands—maybe give her a hug—but this wave of uncertainty would be gone by morning. Her feisty personality would return, and she wouldn't remember the hug too fondly.

"I still don't like the idea of you staying alone. Not with a killer on the loose."

Fierce independence replaced the uncertainty in her eyes, and she jerked her hands free. "I was a cop, Mitch. I know how to protect myself."

"I know you do, but you're upset and not thinking straight."

"You're right. I'm upset. Of course, I'm upset. I lay right next to my friend's body. But don't think that means I'm fall-

ing apart. I'm thinking clearly, and I'll be fine on my own."
Her shoulders jerked higher.

He wasn't going to get anywhere with her. He had no
choice but to back off. But he wouldn't leave her unprotected.
He'd arrange for an officer to sit outside all night.

"You're tired. I should be going." He started to rise.

"Wait." She grabbed his arm stopping him. "We haven't
talked about the investigation."

"What about it?"

"I want to be part of it."

He should've known this was coming and prepared a way
to say no without hurting her more. "You know I can't do
that. You're a civilian now and the closest thing we have to
a witness."

"No one needs to know I'm helping."

He opened his mouth to object but she jumped on it.

"You know Tommy will agree." She crossed her arms as
if she felt it necessary to defend herself from his questioning
gaze. She didn't, though.

He was the one who needed defending from these eyes im-
ploring him to give in. Spending time with the one woman
who'd gotten beyond his defenses and made him almost agree
to date a coworker wasn't a wise move.

"I can't let you help, Kat, without jeopardizing my job."

"What if you were me?" she asked, her eyes going wide.
"What would you want?"

"Wouldn't matter what I wanted, it's what I'd make sure
happened."

"Exactly. You'd make sure you were included in the investigation. I'm just trying to do the same thing." She put a hand
on his arm and the warmth of her touch melted his resolve.

Having her by his side would be a good thing, right? If
she wouldn't let her family surround and protect her from

this killer, if she worked with him, he'd be able to keep an eye on her.

"Please," she said softly, and her big brown eyes pleaded with him.

Eyes he'd once looked into where he'd found the same longing he'd felt in his own heart before hurting her. He couldn't do it again. He'd let her work on the case, but he'd lay down some ground rules. "You don't call any of the shots. You're just an observer. You got it?"

"I got it." She squeezed his arm and smiled. "Thanks."

He nodded, keeping his look neutral even though he liked the warmth of her hand on his arm.

"So where should we begin?" she asked.

Her sudden enthusiasm made him smile. "It's late. We'll start first thing in the morning."

"No!" The word shot out like a bullet. "If I bring you up to speed on what I know about Nathan, we can hit the ground running in the morning."

Staying for a few more minutes wouldn't be a problem, right? "Tell me what you've done so far."

"I started by investigating Nathan Bodig. Everything about the man checks out. He was an all-around good guy, and I couldn't find any obvious reason why someone would want to kill him."

"What'd he do for a living?" Mitch picked up his cup and took a long sip.

"Social worker for the Oregon Department of Human Services. He worked with kids at risk. Monitoring them at home and placing them in foster homes."

"So he dealt with troubled families and might've made someone mad. Wouldn't be the first time someone in a position like his was threatened."

She nodded. "I was going to talk to his coworkers, but I

hadn't gotten that far yet. With your credentials we'll have better access to them."

She so desperately wanted to find Nancy's killer that she was rushing ahead. As they worked the case, he'd need to keep an eye out for that and make sure they stayed on solid footing. "I'd like to hold off on that until we have evidence that proves the crash wasn't an accident."

"You doubt it?"

"Nancy's death could have nothing to do with her brother's, and I don't want to jump to conclusions." She appeared to get upset with his reluctance to embrace her theory so he moved on before she argued. "Where exactly did the accident occur?"

"On Highway 30 near Clatskanie. Nathan was dating a woman he met at a conference. She lives in Astoria and he was on the way to visit her."

"And you checked her out, too?"

"She's as squeaky clean as Nathan. She was the one who reported Nathan missing. When he didn't show up as scheduled, she tried calling him. After a few tries with no answer, she contacted Nancy. Nancy set out, planning to retrace his route, but by that time, a trucker had spotted the car burning in the ravine and called it in."

Good. At least Kat hadn't let her emotions keep her from following strong investigative techniques. If Nathan really had been murdered, then the girlfriend would be a prime suspect and someone they'd need to scrutinize. He was glad Kat had already gotten the basic story—it was a place to start. "You talk with the officer who investigated the accident?"

"That would be Senior Trooper Ed Franklin. I tried to talk with him, but he shut me down." She crossed her arms. "He said I was no longer a police officer and I'd have to go through proper channels for my information."

"He was just following protocol, Kat."

"You and I both know he could've helped me if he wanted to." She ended with an adorable little pout that kicked up his pulse, and he knew it was time for him to get out of there before he did something he'd regret.

"Well, he won't have a choice with me." He stood and headed for the door before she tried to stop him again. "We'll start with him first thing tomorrow."

She rushed ahead as if she thought he was going to change his mind about including her in the investigation and wanted him to leave before he said anything to that effect. Now that her pleading expression had disappeared and he could think straight, he wanted to do just that.

She shrugged out of his jacket and handed it to him with a sweet smile.

The softness took him by surprise. She'd always been so tough. So independent. Not needing anyone. The very reasons he'd been attracted to her. But this vulnerable side of her tugged at something in him that he'd only felt for his family and Lori. He wanted to protect Kat. To take care of her. But that wasn't the end of his interest and the rest wasn't at all familial.

He took the jacket and stepped outside. "Tommy and I'll pick you up at nine. Make sure you lock the door."

He heard her snort as he walked away and a smile found his lips. She was starting to get a bit of her spunk back. Good. With a killer running free, she'd need every bit of her determination and then some to stay alive.

THREE

Morning sun filtered through the blinds as Kat laid her Bible on the table and got up to see if Mitch and Tommy had arrived yet. Her usual morning devotions reminded her to let go of her fear. God was here, by her side. Walking before her, beside her. He would take care of her.

Just not those you love, huh, Kat? The thought came from deep inside, and she squelched it. She trusted God. She just wanted to help Him to make sure things didn't go wrong.

She scissored opened the blinds and saw the same squad car she'd spotted when she'd peeked outside around 3:00 a.m. after a noise woke her. Not a pleasant discovery. Tommy knew how she detested her birth father's iron control, and she rarely tolerated people making decisions for her. So it had to have been Mitch. Still, she wouldn't ask them to cancel the unit. Her siblings would be more likely to keep their distance if they thought provisions had been made for her safety.

She let the blinds fall and pressed her only sister's speed dial number.

"Hello," Dani answered on the fifth ring, sounding sleepy.

"Hey," Kat said, trying to be cheerful though the loss of her friend weighed heavy on her heart. "I have something I need to tell you about."

"Does it have to be this early in the morning?" Dani was so not a morning person.

"Sorry, but it does." Kat launched into a description of the attack and Nancy's death.

"Thanks for calling me last night." Her sarcastic reply hurt, but Kat deserved it and more for shutting out her sister. "Are you okay?"

"Fine, and I'm sorry about last night. I couldn't very well tell you about this and ask you not to tell the others. Then everyone would rush over here, and I couldn't handle that."

"So no one else knows?"

"No."

"You should've called Cole first. You know how mad he'll be when he finds out this happened and you spent the night alone."

Cole was the last person Kat wanted to tell. With their oldest brother, Ethan, on a month-long honeymoon, the usually quiet Cole had taken charge and was very vocal of late.

"That's why I need your help," Kat said. "He'll want to take me off this case and keep me under lock and key until the killer's caught."

"And you don't think he should do that."

"I have to work on this case, Dani. Nancy was my friend. Plus I screwed up and have to prove myself or I'll never be in charge again."

"I don't know, sis."

"C'mon, Dani." She used her most persuasive tone. "With the way Ethan and Cole want us both to sit behind desks all the time, you of all people should back me up on this." She and Dani had fought their brothers treating them like helpless females instead of trained law enforcement officials for two years now. Their brothers had only recently started letting them get more involved, but this situation would make them pull back.

"You have a point," Dani said, although grudgingly.

Kat almost had her cooperation. "I've already gotten approval to work with the detectives in charge of the case so I'll spend most of my time with them. They've also posted an officer outside my door for when I'm home. I'll be perfectly safe."

"I'm not sure this is a good idea...."

"Please, Dani. I need to do this."

She sighed. "You're sure you'll be okay?"

"Yes. I'm positive."

"Fine. I'll tell Cole about it when I get to work, and I'll try to convince him to stay away. But don't blame me if he comes after you."

"Thanks, Dani. I owe you one." The doorbell rang, and Kat jumped. "Tommy's at the door. I gotta go."

"Tommy. Wait. This means you're working with Mitch Elliot, too. When were you planning on telling me about that?"

Never. "I'll call you later." Kat hung up before her sister, who knew all about Mitch's rejection, had a chance to grill her.

She went to the door and found Mitch leaning on the wall, his legs crossed at the ankle. Her heart did a little free fall as she tipped her head back and ran her gaze up the strong column of his neck to meet his eyes. She was rewarded for the effort with a slow smile spreading across a rugged face with a hint of stubble to match his dark hair. He wore boot-cut jeans, a white dress shirt and tie covered with the same Portland Police Bureau windbreaker as last night. The memory of his scent as the jacket circled her in warmth still lingered in her mind and she had to take a deep breath to clear it out.

"Where's Tommy?" she asked and stepped back as the ramifications of spending the day alone with him sunk in.

"He's taking care of something, and he'll meet us later." The only reason Mitch would be so vague on Tommy's whereabouts was if they thought it would bother her, making it easy to guess his location. "So he's at the morgue?"

"Yeah."

She appreciated the two of them trying to spare her from the gruesome details, but she couldn't let them continue to tiptoe around her. "You guys don't need to treat me with kid gloves, Mitch."

"Okay," he said, and something that looked suspiciously like relief flared in his eyes for a brief moment.

She got it. He didn't want to be burdened with her fragility brought on by grief. She'd have to make a point today of showing him she could do her job no matter her pain. And that started with making sure Nancy's parents had been notified of her death.

"Has anyone located Nancy's parents?" she asked.

"They're meeting Tommy at the morgue right now."

So they were at the viewing window for the second time in a few months identifying their child. Kat couldn't imagine their pain. She offered a quick prayer for them before looking back at Mitch. "I didn't know them, but I'd like to offer my condolences. I don't suppose you'd break the rules and give me their contact information."

"We can get it from Tommy when we meet up with him." He sounded as sad as she felt. "Trooper Franklin's expecting us so we should get going."

"I just need to grab my stuff from upstairs and then I'm ready to go." She nodded at the kitchen. "There's fresh coffee. Help yourself."

As she ran up the stairs, she heard his phone ringing. Maybe it was Tommy calling from the autopsy to give them a lead. At least she hoped so. The sooner they got a few strong leads the faster they'd solve the murder and bring closure to Nancy's family.

She secured her gun in the holster and slipped it onto her

belt then gathered her things and retraced her steps. On the landing, she paused and looked down at Mitch. She'd expected to find him in the kitchen getting coffee. Instead, he stood leaning on the fireplace mantel, one hand on his cell, one massaging the back of his neck as if his conversation was tense. She studied him. His broad shoulders and long lean body. His self-assured stance.

A man this attractive should have women flocking around him, but if rumors were true, he didn't even date. Of course, she didn't, either. But at thirty she had a few more years than he had to find a mate if she ever chose to do so. He was at least four years older, maybe five.

He turned, looking up at her. His gaze roved from her head to her toes and back up again. Her heart dipped, and she pressed her nails into her palms to keep from embarrassing herself by fawning over him.

She wouldn't let him get to her again. The loss of her adoptive parents had made her look back on her life and take stock of all she'd been through. To remember all the horrible things that had happened so they couldn't be repeated. And that meant not letting a man get close enough to control and hurt her as her mother had been hurt. Even a man like Mitch, who on the surface seemed like an upstanding kind of guy.

Just keep remembering that, Kat, and you'll be fine.

She continued down the stairs and by the time she reached him, he was saying goodbye.

"Tommy," he said, without making her pump him for information as she'd expected. "The drug in the syringe was propofol."

Propofol. Very dangerous and deadly in the wrong hands. "The anesthesia drug used in surgeries," she said, trying to keep the renewed fear out of her tone.

"If he'd injected you with the entire syringe, your breathing would've been severely compromised."

"And I'd be dead," she said in a whisper.

"Nancy's tox screen was positive, as well," he said quickly, as if wanting to move on.

Kat wished she could let go of her memories of that night as easily. It'd be a long time before she stopped seeing Nancy lying there next to her while the killer tried to end her life, too.

"The M.E. estimates Nancy had been dead less than an hour before he arrived on scene," he continued.

"Not long after she called me," Kat said and clenched her hands to fight back a fresh wave of sorrow. If only she'd gotten to Nancy sooner. Or taken her more seriously when she'd claimed Nathan had been murdered. Her friend could still be alive.

"Still, the killer could've gotten away if he'd wanted to leave." Mitch paused for a long moment and made eye contact. "Sounds like your theory may be right. He knew you were coming and waited for you to arrive so he could kill you."

"Then he'll likely try again." She stated the obvious and hated how it made her breathe faster to ward off her fear.

Mitch searched her face, his intriguing eyes softened as he moved closer. He took her chin between his fingers and turned her head, studying her like a bug under a microscope.

"Your nose may be broken. We'll make time today to get it checked out." He sounded so clinical, which was the farthest thing from what she was feeling.

"I'm fine." She gazed up at him. He was so close she could feel his breath on her cheek.

With his other hand, he gently brushed his thumb over her cheekbone. "You never said how this happened. Did you fall and hit the floor?"

"The killer punched me."

He hissed out a breath and his thumb trailed down her cheek and under her chin, sending every nerve in her body into awareness. Even the scientific way he'd held her chin felt good. It was almost like a caress, wrapping her with warmth. Warmth she had no business feeling if she was going to keep Mitch at bay, much less stay alert and out of the path of a killer.

Mitch didn't know what it was about Kat that got to him. Sure, she was cute, adorable even. A brown-eyed, curly-haired, five foot four bundle of adorable, but he'd resisted adorable in the past.

He was probably reacting to what had happened to her last night, but man, when she'd told him their suspect punched her, he'd seen red. Bright, vivid, bull-fighting red and he had to touch her. To connect with her on some level. So he'd used her injury as an excuse to reach out to her. Soon, he felt the anger melt and something else he didn't want to think about replaced it. It had lingered ever since.

Even now after a sixty-minute drive on winding Oregon roads, he couldn't get images of her being manhandled out of his head when he should be focusing on a case that wouldn't solve itself.

Maybe things would be better once Tommy joined them. And maybe if they talked for the rest of the drive, his mind would stop wandering to places it had no business going.

"So do you ever miss being a cop?" he asked, trying to sound casually interested.

"Sometimes." She faced the window as if trying to shut him down.

"But you like working with the agency?"

"Most of the time."

Great. A real talker. "What don't you like about it?"

"It can be difficult to work with family."

With his parents dead and his only sibling wandering the streets of Portland, he couldn't begin to understand that, but he knew her family was important to her.

"How so?" he asked and took a long sip of the rich coffee they'd poured into travel mugs before leaving her house.

She shrugged.

"C'mon, Kat. Would it hurt to talk to me?"

She swiveled and searched his face with big brown eyes. Sweet eyes. Eyes with no residual frustration but were just filled with questions. "Why do you want to be so buddy buddy all of a sudden?"

"You've been through something horrible, and I thought it might help to talk."

She just looked at him, her expression unreadable.

"This isn't about that crush you had on me, is it?" he asked.

She rolled her eyes.

"Sorry for bringing it up, but there are a lot of female officers in the department who don't exactly like to see me."

She frowned at him, and he got the message. She didn't feel the least bit sorry for him. Something he should expect coming from one of the women he'd rejected, but for some odd reason it was important that she understood.

"It's a problem, Kat. A very real one." He waited for a response but got none. "You try doing your job when half the force is hurt because you wouldn't go out with them."

She snorted.

"What?" he asked.

"Half the force?"

"Fine." He grinned at her teasing tone. "I exaggerated."

Her lips twitched in a smile. "In all seriousness, I heard other officers complaining about how hurt they were when you rejected them. I know it's a problem for you."

"I appreciate your understanding."

"I can be sympathetic now, but make no mistake, I was mad at you. Or maybe I was more embarrassed that you shut me down in front of my coworkers. But all of that's in the past." Her smile faded. "It's not important anymore. Nothing seems quite as important after losing Nancy that way."

The opening he hoped for. "You want to talk about what happened?"

She shrugged.

"I've been there, Kat. Not the being attacked part, but I lost a partner once."

Her eyes flew up to his, surprise brightening the color. "Really? I hadn't heard about that."

"It happened in Salem. Before I moved here." He looked at her wondering if he should go on. If he did, he'd expose feelings he never shared. Raw feelings that he'd rather keep to himself, but he could help her. "It's something you never get over. I'm still trying to let it go."

She peered at him then, her eyes soft. Vulnerable. The emotions from last night were present and vivid on her face.

"Do you feel guilty?" she asked.

Her whisper-soft voice cut into him and once again, he was back *there,* with Lori the day she'd been shot, stuck in the scene that had replayed in his mind too many times to count. The bright sunshine. The deafening sound of a shotgun as the man bolted out of his house and opened fire. The sticky blood everywhere at once. A bullet slicing into his neck, spinning him to the ground where he was powerless to help Lori—not only his partner but the woman he'd just asked to marry him.

"You know," Kat added, oblivious to his turmoil. "Guilty, as if you could've prevented it from happening?"

"It's not as if we have any control over what happens." He stopped, not trusting himself to say anything until he took a few deep breaths. "No matter what I do if God allows people I care about to be hurt, I can't stop it." His voice was heavy with sadness, and he saw the same thing on Kat's face. "I wish I could go back to the days when I believed God heard my prayers."

She didn't respond immediately, but sat there as if gathering her thoughts. "It may be hard to see at times, Mitch, but God does listen, and He has a good plan for your life."

He glanced at her again. "After all you've been through and seen on the job, you honestly believe that?"

"I may not like what He allows to happen, but I know He's there."

"It would be nice to feel that way. I just can't," he said with such finality that she looked away, and he was left with his thoughts again.

Thoughts of his sister, Angie. Every day, he expected to arrive at a homicide scene only to discover she was the victim. He tried not to think about it. Tried, but failed every time he caught a case. Every time he had to inform a victim's family that their loved one would not be coming home. Every time he worked his leads and brought a killer to justice.

And even times like now, as he parked in front of the Oregon State Police office in St. Helens, he knew when he talked to the officer about Bodig's death, a part of him could easily slip into questions about why God took Nathan Bodig. Questions that brought no answers.

He turned off the engine and as Kat started to get out, his mind moved to the upcoming meeting. "I'd appreciate it if you'd remember you're just an observer here. Especially since Franklin's already proved he plays by the rules."

"I'll try," she said and slipped out of the car.

He followed her into the crisp morning air and paused by the office door to enjoy a rare sun break. As usual for February in Oregon, by the time they came back outside the sun would most likely have retreated behind gray clouds.

He opened the door for Kat and followed her inside where a young clerk escorted them through a bullpen area to a desk in the back. A stout, uniformed male came to his feet, his eyes roving over Kat, then Mitch, taking in details an officer of the law was trained to see.

"Senior Trooper Ed Franklin." He thrust out a hand.

Mitch offered his business card while completing introductions.

"You didn't mention Ms. Justice would be accompanying you." His tone hinted at opposition.

Mitch eyed up the officer with a stare he'd perfected in suspect interrogations. "Is that a problem?"

"No," he said, though Mitch heard the reluctance in the single word. He sat and gestured toward chairs by his cluttered desk. "So you came to talk about the Bodig fatality."

Mitch waited for Kat to sit then took the other chair. "I'm interested in hearing how you determined this crash was an accident."

"First off, a crash like Bodig's isn't unusual for that stretch of highway." Franklin leaned back in his chair and clasped his hands behind his neck. He seemed relaxed but Mitch could see he remained alert. "We've covered several fatal accidents in that location. Second, it was a rainy night with slick roads."

"So you think visibility might've been a factor in the crash?" Mitch clarified.

"Could be." He snapped forward and pulled out a map, pointing to a section of Highway 30. "This is where it happened. Deep ravines line both sides of the road here. It wouldn't take much of a misstep to turn fatal."

"Any possibility he was forced off the road?"

"There were no skid marks at the scene. So that would be highly unlikely. But without an eye witness, I can't be one hundred percent positive."

"No skid marks?" Kat asked, clearly surprised.

"None."

Interesting. A lack of skid marks would mean Nathan

didn't apply his brakes to keep from going off the road. But that wasn't conclusive. His brakes could've been cut, or Bodig could have been impaired. Maybe by alcohol or drugs or he fell asleep. "What about Bodig? Did you check him out?"

"We ran down the usual profile. Blood alcohol, tox screen, D.M.V. record. All clean. He made the trip every weekend to visit his fiancée in Astoria. From what she and his sister both said, he'd been burning the candle at both ends. My best guess is that he fell asleep at the wheel."

"And no unusual findings on the vehicle?"

"Unusual? No. But it was seriously charred." He shook his head. "Don't know how long it burned before the fire department arrived on scene. A trucker spotted the wreck and called it in."

"Do you know what happened to the vehicle after it was released?" Mitch asked, hoping they could get a look at it.

Franklin opened a drawer and pulled out a sheet of paper. He circled something in the middle of the page and slid it across the desk. "This is the tow company we recommend to next of kin. Henry down there is good about helping them dispose of vehicles. You can check with them."

"Thanks," Mitch said. "One more thing. Bodig's cell phone. It was never recovered."

"His sister said that was odd so we spent extra time looking for it." He reclined again. "With all the windows shattered in the car, his phone could've been ejected and landed anywhere. The brush is too thick to search every inch."

"But it definitely wasn't in the car," Kat added.

He nodded and looked at Mitch. "You mind telling me what this's all about?"

"We think this may not have been an accident."

"Suppose you tell me what you're basing that on." This time he didn't mask his defensive tone.

"Relax. It has nothing to do with your investigation. His

sister was murdered after she started looking into the accident."

"Murdered." Franklin's feet came to the floor with a loud thud. "Why didn't you tell me that right up front?"

"I needed to know your mind-set at the time of the investigation. Telling you could've changed your perception of things."

"You think?" He kept shaking his head. "Now I'm wondering if I missed something. How'd the sister die?"

"Injected with propofol."

"If Bodig had taken propofol, he couldn't have been driving," Franklin mumbled to himself then a light-bulb-gone-off look brightened his face. "This's why you want to see the car. You think it was tampered with."

"It's possible." Mitch said, not wanting to get into details of their investigation with Franklin. "We'd appreciate a copy of the accident report as soon as possible."

"I'll run one off right now." Franklin got up. "Be right back."

When he was out of hearing distance, Mitch faced Kat. "Not what you expected to hear?"

"No, but the lack of skid marks aren't conclusive. He still could've been murdered." Her chin jutted out in a cute defiant angle.

"Agreed. If our killer has access to propofol, he could get any number of drugs that didn't show up on the basic tox screen Franklin had run. If Bodig had drugs on board it would've seriously hindered his ability to drive." He smiled to try to ease the concern wedged on her face. "But we'll need solid evidence before we can request additional tests."

"Question is where are we going to find that evidence?"

"You up for a road trip?"

"Where to?"

"The accident scene." He felt the excitement of the hunt raising his pulse and heard it settling in his voice.

"Absolutely," she agreed. "Though after two months it seems unlikely there'd be anything for us to find."

"It's still a good idea to get a visual of how things went down. After that we'll take a look at Bodig's vehicle." He saw Franklin returning, so ended their conversation.

"Here you go." Franklin handed over the file.

"Thanks." Mitch stood. "Mind if we take your map?"

"Not at all." Franklin picked it up and gave it to him.

"You've got my card. Call me if you think of anything that might help."

Franklin gave a clipped nod. "Will do."

Mitch gestured for Kat to precede him, and they headed for the exit.

"By the way, I meant to say thanks in there," he said, slipping ahead and holding the door for her.

"For what?"

"For letting me do most of the talking."

"Don't get used to it." She grinned up at him, revealing small dimples in both cheeks.

He ignored the way his heart dipped again and followed her outside.

The sun had given way to rain. More than a drizzle, less than a steady rain. Kat flipped up her hood. Mitch's P.P.B. windbreaker didn't have one, so he rushed ahead and unlocked the doors.

In the car, he handed over the paper from Franklin. "Can you call the garage to see if the wreck is still there or if they got rid of it for salvage?"

"Sure."

He headed out of town, and she dug out her phone. On Highway 30, he paid close attention to the two-lane road. With slick rain, the road could be as dangerous as Franklin had indicated. Kat chatted with the tow company, and he could tell by her questions that they no longer had Bodig's vehicle.

"The car's at a salvage yard." She dialed another number. "Let's pray it hasn't been crushed for scrap yet."

She was right. They should pray. But then he should pray all the time. He just couldn't seem to manage it. He'd held on to his faith when his dad died just after Mitch turned fifteen, and when Angie turned to drugs. He'd even kept praying after his mom's death. But when Lori was gunned down and everyone he'd ever loved was taken from him, he knew God no longer cared for him or those he loved. So he'd shut himself off from other people and from God.

But if what Kat said earlier was true, maybe he'd been wrong. Maybe God was still there. And maybe He'd brought Kat into his life again to show him that.

He glanced at her as she concentrated while a rumbling male voice barked at her over the phone. The little bit of a woman holding her own with the surly man brought a smile to his lips.

"How can you not know if the vehicle is there?" Frustration bit into her tone and she took several deep breaths. What followed was kinder, softer. As if she remembered she could get more cooperation using honey. And she could. At least with him. With her sweet tone feeling like a soft smile, resisting her was going to be harder than he first thought.

Seriously, Elliot. You're acting like an adolescent boy.

He rolled his eyes at his behavior and caught sight in the rearview mirror of a white van fast approaching. He took a better look. Spotted a logo on the hood. Blinked and looked again. The same van as last night.

Nancy's killer was following them.

Mitch didn't want to panic Kat so he didn't say anything but kept an eye on the van. As they reached a narrow turn, the vehicle sped up and the driver gunned the engine.

They were approaching Bodig's accident site. If their theory was right, the killer had drugged Bodig and forced him off the road. Maybe the driver had the same plans for the two of them, minus the drugs.

"You need to get off the phone," Mitch said with urgency.

She cupped her hand over it. "I'll just be another minute."

He looked up again. The van was now only a few car lengths behind. "A minute's too long."

"What's going on?"

He jerked his head toward the rearview mirror. "You need to brace yourself. It looks like Nancy's killer is about to run us off the road."

FOUR

Kat swiveled to look out the back window. A full-size white van zoomed closer. His powerful engine roared in her ears as they climbed higher into the misty rain. She craned her neck to get a clear look of the driver, but the rain obscured her view. Still, she heard him coming closer.

Was he really planning to run them off the road? To kill them?

Father, please, no! Don't let this happen.

Mitch careened the car around a curve, tires slipping on the wet pavement, spitting rain in all directions. They skidded wildly, tossing them into the path of a massive logging truck.

The driver laid on his air horn, and Kat's heart rate shot higher. Mitch fought with the wheel, and she felt him ease off the gas. With a jerk, they came out of the skid and the truck roared past them, too close for comfort. Mitch blew out a breath and slowed even more while she took a quick look behind.

The van was still there. Closer now.

She glanced back at Mitch. His eyes were focused on the road, his jaw firmed.

"You have a plan or are we just going to try to outrun him?" She was surprised at how calm she sounded when her heart was thumping an erratic beat in her chest.

"His vehicle's bigger, and he could easily send us off the road." He switched on the wipers, the intermittent swish across the windshield ending with a shudder on dry glass. "It's better to slow and come to a stop near a guardrail."

She took a quick look out the side window. Deep ravines, thick brush and huge pines waited to claim their car and potentially their lives. His plan seemed like the best option. Still they needed help.

"I'll call for backup." She dialed 911 and relayed their situation, trying to keep her voice calm and measured as Mitch continued to slow the vehicle.

The van was close enough that she heard the rhythmic *thump, thump, thump* of his wipers. Only moments to impact now. Kat grabbed the seat and braced herself.

The van slammed into their car. Metal shrieked against metal as their tires dropped onto the shoulder. Kat jolted forward and planted a hand on the dashboard. Mitch jerked the wheel and the car lurched back onto the road, gravel spraying from all sides.

"Plan B?" she asked, nearly breathless.

"This is still our best option." He continued to slow, the speedometer reading forty-five. Forty. Thirty-five. Thirty.

The van was backing off, but there was no time to let down her guard. He could simply be falling back to gain enough speed to ram them again.

"I'll pull over up ahead. We can take cover behind the guardrail." Mitch slowed even more. "Ready?"

"As ready as I'll ever be."

"When I come to a stop, get out of here. Don't waste any time. Leave your door open and I'll be right behind you."

The car jerked to a stop, and she didn't wait for him to shift into Park but bolted out. The cold metal of the guardrail bit into her hands as she catapulted over. Her feet slid on the wet grass and she hit the ground on her hip, the pungent scent of moist earth rising up to greet her. She came to her knees and drew her weapon to cover Mitch as he lunged out of the vehicle. He tumbled to a stop beside her and gracefully moved into a crouch.

The van slowed, now crawling closer. The black windshield reflected gray clouds obstructing her view of the driver. She watched and waited. Her breath coming in short little pulses of vapor disappearing into the cooler air.

She glanced at Mitch. Rain plastered thick locks of hair onto his forehead and molded his jacket to his large shoulders. The intensity in his eyes and face reassuring as he held his weapon in steady hands. If a killer was going to hunt her down, Mitch was a formidable ally.

The van slowed to a crawl and then stopped. The driver revved the engine, thick white exhaust rising up and mixing with the mist as the vehicle vibrated under the restraint of the brakes.

"What do you think he's doing?" she asked, a shiver making its way down her body.

"Not a clue." Mitch looked around. "But be ready to move if he heads for us."

A sudden roar of the van's engine split the silence and tires squealed into motion. Slipping, sliding, the vehicle picked up speed, racing their way. Kat shifted, moving to her feet. The van roared up the road, tires hissing over the wet pavement as the odor of burning rubber filled the air.

"Doesn't look like he's coming for us," Mitch said, his eyes never moving from the van. "Try to get that plate if he passes by."

Kat's heart thundered in her chest, but she stayed put and kept her focus on the vehicle. Twenty feet away. Picking up speed. Now fifteen. She saw the shadow of the driver as he seemed to be changing positions.

What was he doing?

His arm came up.

"Gun," Mitch shouted as he went airborne and in the next moment they were both on the ground, his body covering hers.

A shot ricocheted through the trees. Then another one. The car window exploded in fragments pelting down on them. She was vaguely aware of soggy leaves and pine needles pressed into her face as Mitch's heavy weight flattened her into the ground. A third shot pinged off the guardrail and slammed in the dirt with a thump.

The van sideswiped their car, sliding Mitch's smaller vehicle into the rail. Metal ground against metal as the guardrail crumbled into a tangled mess and groaned toward them. Mitch shifted, circling his arms around her and rolling them out of the way. Tires continued to slide, coming to a stop inches from her eyes.

More shots. Closer now. *Pop. Pop. Pop.*

Mitch tightened his hold, and she felt his heart thumping against her back. A sure steady rhythm, but fast. She didn't move. Couldn't move. She lay there waiting for the shooter to get out and train his gun on them. But the mighty engine revved and climbed the hill, the sound disappearing like a shadow in the mist.

"Are you hit?" Mitch asked, his breath stirring her hair.

"No." She shuddered out a breath and took in another. "You?"

"I'm good." He lifted his head. "Stay down." He pulled his arms free and swiftly came to his knees.

Cold air assaulted her, and she felt vulnerable. She wanted to pull him back down, but rolled to the side instead. He'd moved to the end of the twisted guardrail and poked his head up. "He's gone."

Her breath hitched, and she felt as if she might lose it. She had to get a grip. Let Mitch know that she was stronger than this timid woman he'd seen since yesterday. She concentrated on breathing.

They were alive. Safe. Both of them.

Thank You, God.

"You okay, Kat?"

She gave a clipped nod. "God was watching out for us."

"If you say so."

"Hey," she said. "You're not being fair. If you blame God when bad things happen then you're admitting He's in charge. And that means He should get the credit for good things, too."

He arched a brow and studied her for a few moments. "Not sure nearly losing our lives is a good thing, but point taken." He climbed over the guardrail and checked out the car. "It's not drivable so we can't pursue him. I'll radio in an update on his location."

He holstered his weapon and went to the driver's side. The door wrenched open with a nerve-racking groan disturbing the quiet. Kat pulled herself up using the mangled guardrail. This could've been her. Him. Both of them. Twisted beyond repair.

She shuddered again and stretched, easing out kinks while checking for injuries. She felt blood congealed next to her ear. She remembered hitting a stick when Mitch tackled her. The injury didn't feel serious, but she'd have a bunch of bruises. At least she hadn't been shot. Perhaps thanks to Mitch. She went to stand beside his door to listen in on his conversation.

He looked up at her. "You sure you're okay?"

She nodded but didn't say anything. Her thoughts were too jumbled to speak. All that mattered was that they were safe for now. At least until the killer tried to end her life again.

Mitch should be paying attention to Trooper Franklin's comments about the paint transferred from the van to his department-issued car, but his eyes kept drifting to Kat. She hadn't said a word in quite a while, and he was starting to worry about her.

He'd asked if she wanted to talk, but she'd clammed up and sat on the end of the guardrail that was still intact, her arms around her waist as she waited for the troopers to finish their report. Her eyes were unreadable, but there was no doubt she was really shaken up. And she should be. Two attempts on her life in as many days would unsettle the best cop.

He was still flustered, too. They'd barely made it out alive. His car could've plunged into a ravine with them in it, either one of them could've taken a bullet or been crushed by the sliding vehicle.

"You with me, Elliot?" Franklin asked, his eyes appraising.

Mitch nodded. "You'll have the car towed to the state police crime lab so they can process the paint transferred from the van."

"Right. We should be able to get the manufacturer, make and the year manufactured from the transfer. That combined with the three digits you caught of the plate the other day and maybe you'll find your suspect."

"You deal with the state lab often?"

"Enough, why?"

"Just wondered about the time frame for results."

"Seventy-two hours at the soonest. Probably longer."

Three days. Three days during which Mitch needed to make sure he kept Kat out of the killer's sights. She didn't know it yet, but she wasn't going home tonight. No matter how strong-willed and independent she was, he would insist she spend the night with one of her siblings or at his house. He'd prefer she chose the siblings so that wounded expression didn't make him do something dumb like hold her and promise everything would be okay.

That was an empty promise if he ever made one. Nothing was ever all right. Nothing. He ought to know that by now.

"I need to wait until someone from the lab gets here," Franklin continued. "But Trooper Smith is ready to leave if you want a ride to your rental car."

"Thanks. I'll get Ms. Justice." It felt odd calling her anything other than Kat, but he didn't want to draw attention to their personal connection.

He skirted around his damaged car and swiped his hair off his forehead. A steady rain hissed down on them and, although the troopers gave them both slickers, a gusting wind had blown his hood off so many times that he finally gave up and left it down.

As he approached, Kat looked up, revealing wet curls clinging to her neck. They looked cold against her creamy skin. He was temped to peel them free so he shoved his hands in his pockets instead. "We can catch a ride with the trooper."

She eased off the guardrail and groaned. "You as sore as I am?"

"No, but I wasn't assaulted last night." He slipped a hand on the slick plastic of the poncho covering her arm and directed her across the road. She didn't shake off his hand and that told him a great deal about her mood. He settled her in the front seat and climbed in the back.

The trooper tried to make conversation with her, but she gave him one-word answers, and he finally stopped trying. As a former law enforcement officer, she was probably still running through the incident, trying to see if they could've handled it better. He was doing the same thing. He was confident they'd made the best of a bad situation, but he was uneasy about the gun. When he'd bailed from the car, he'd thought the vehicle was their only exposure and hadn't expected the suspect to pull a weapon and open fire.

The gun brought things to a whole new level. One they'd have to face head-on until this guy was caught. Mitch and Tommy were up to the task of protecting Kat, but it wouldn't hurt to have help. When they got a moment alone, even though she was against involving her family in this, he'd suggest they do just that.

When the trooper pulled up to a service station with a car rental sign out front, Mitch leaned forward. "You mind if Ms. Justice waits here while I get the keys?"

"No problem," Smith answered.

"I'll be right back." Mitch hopped out and filled out the paperwork for a small sedan, got directions to the salvage yard then went out the side door into rain that seemed to be letting up.

In the car, he shrugged out of his poncho and cranked up the heat so by the time he pulled up beside the trooper, warm air was flowing at his feet.

Kat climbed in and struggled to get out of her slicker, the vinyl squeaking in protest.

"Want help with that?" he asked.

"I'm not fragile, you know." She sounded mad about something, but he couldn't see her face under the poncho to make sure. She ripped the poncho free and eyed him up for long moments. A hint of a spark had returned to her eyes, and he could see she was getting her spunk back.

He couldn't help but grin at her tenacious spirit, but she didn't return his smile. Instead, her gaze turned challenging—almost defiant. Much the way she'd looked at him when he'd said he didn't date coworkers. But then she'd let him have it and now she clamped down on her lips.

"What's wrong?" he asked.

"Nothing." She seemed sincere, but he knew her well enough to know she had something on her mind, and she didn't plan to share it with him. At least not yet. He couldn't drag it out of her. She'd tell him when she was ready.

"Are you still up for the salvage yard before we meet Tommy for an update?" he asked, moving on.

"Of course."

"The guy inside said the place is a few miles down the road." He backed the car out and eased onto the main thoroughfare where traffic was light. He felt her eyes remain on him, but resisted the urge to look at her.

She fidgeted and shifted in the seat several times before finally turning to him. "You saved my neck back there, Mitch. Thank you." She might've said thank you, but she sounded disgruntled over having to say it.

He glanced at her. "Not that I need gratitude, but that wasn't exactly a hearty thank-you."

"But I meant it."

"So why the tone?"

"If you were with Tommy and this happened would you have jumped on top of him?"

Her description brought an odd picture to his mind, and he chuckled. "Pretty sure Tommy would deck me if I tried."

"Exactly."

"So you're saying thank you, but you really mean back off."

"No… I mean…" She shrugged. "I don't know. I appreciate the thought that you would want to protect me, but after years of having to prove myself as a cop just because I'm a woman, it just sits wrong with me. Now it's the same with my brothers. They think anything dangerous has to be done by a man." She looked down at her hands. "It's like none of you really trust women to have your back."

"It was just an instinct, Kat. I didn't think about it. I just acted." He gave her a long look. "But that doesn't mean I don't trust you or your abilities. Tommy tells me you were a great cop. If you were still on the force, I'd partner with you without a second thought."

She didn't say anything. He looked at her and smiled again. "Are we okay?"

"Yes."

"Speaking of your brothers…" He paused when her shoulders went up. She was going to shut him down. Still he had to try. "Perhaps it's time we bring them in on this."

"Not an option." That protective look from earlier when they'd talked about the fear of loved ones getting hurt claimed her face.

"This isn't about you not wanting them to think you screwed up anymore, is it? You don't want to put them in harm's way."

"No, I don't, and I hope you'll respect my decision to keep it that way."

He wasn't sure how to answer. He didn't need to bring them in on the case right now, but if things escalated, he wanted to keep that option open.

"Mitch," she said. "Promise me you won't talk to them without asking me first."

"I'll leave them out it for now," he answered, and hoped the danger wouldn't reach the point where he'd feel compelled to go against her wishes.

She opened her mouth as if to say something, then closed it and looked out the window. He turned into the salvage yard and pulled up to a ramshackle office building. He reached for his slicker, but the rain hitting the windshield had all but stopped so he left it behind, as did Kat.

"Help you?" An older man with a lip full of chewing tobacco came outside and eyed them suspiciously.

Mitch flashed his badge and the suspicion turned antagonistic.

Kat stepped forward. "Hi. I'm Kat Justice. You must be Mr. Wissler." Her tone was smooth and sultry.

"I am." He let his eyes roam from her head to toe.

Mitch hated how the man leered at her, but the only sign

that she minded was a flicker of her eyes. If he hadn't been watching closely he would've missed that entirely.

"We talked on the phone a few hours ago. I'm looking for the Bodig wreck." She ended with a practiced smile.

Wissler returned it, revealing stained teeth coated with a black liquid. Mitch wanted to shudder at the sight, but Kat simply put her hand on her hip and kept smiling at the guy.

Mitch wasn't sure if he was irritated at her for going all soft and womanly when she'd just lectured him on treating her differently or if he was impressed at how effectively she was working this guy.

"I'm sorry it took us so long to get here. Car trouble." Another smile. "Are we too late?"

"Nah. It's back this way." He lumbered off and a mangy black dog got up and followed.

"Don't say it," Kat whispered.

"Say what?"

"That I just destroyed any point I was trying to make in the car." She gave him an impish smile, and he couldn't help but grin back at her.

They traveled down several narrow aisles toward the back of the yard, his steps lighter from her smile. Something he didn't care to ponder.

Mounds of scrap metal and cars perched precariously at odd angles as if a tornado had come through and tossed them into a heap. A thick coat of rust claimed every item, some were nearly covered in it.

"Here it is." The man pointed at a burned-out shell of a car sitting at the end of a row. "2010 Honda Accord."

"You're sure this is it?" Mitch asked.

Wissler scowled at him then looked at Kat. "I'm positive this is Bodig's car. Only one we've ever had that was torched this bad."

Mitch circled the car, and Kat joined him at the trunk.

His eyes met hers. He could tell she was thinking the same thing. A few hours ago, this could've been their car and they may not have escaped. The thought of Kat trapped in a fiery wreck turned Mitch's stomach and redoubled his resolve to solve this case.

He squatted and ran a hand over the rear panel. He could feel raised chips of paint, maybe left from another vehicle colliding with this one, but they'd long lost their color.

"You see this?" he said, keeping his voice low.

Kat bent down, and he caught a whiff of the same vanilla scent that had nearly distracted him during the shoot-out. He took her fingers and ran them over the spot.

"Are you thinking this is paint from a collision?" she asked.

"I'm not positive, but we're not certain why Bodig ran off the road, so it's worth taking a further look to see if there was another vehicle involved in his accident."

She smiled at him. "Guess we'll be calling the crime lab to pick up another vehicle."

"Hopefully this paint will match the chips left on my car and in a few days, a killer will be behind bars." Mitch stood. "I'll call this in. How about telling Bubba there what we're planning?"

Mitch made the call and watched Kat charm the man as he followed them up to the front. Wissler got a phone call and headed into the building, seeming very reluctant to part with Kat.

A feeling Mitch understood. She was so cute it'd be hard to ignore the softly curling hair, big doelike eyes and a smile— when she used it—that could make his knees weak.

"You ready to go?" he asked after he'd arranged to have the car towed.

She nodded and they headed for the rental.

Once seated, he waited for her to click her seat belt in place. As she bent toward the buckle, her hair fell away, and he spotted a fresh gash running from her ear to her eye along the line of her bruise from last night. Before thinking, he gently lifted her hair out of the way to get a better look.

She jerked back from his touch, and he let his hand fall. She didn't want him to touch her. He shouldn't touch her. But it bothered him all the same. More than he cared to admit. "That happen when I tackled you?"

"Yes, but it's no big deal."

Angry with himself for hurting her, angry with her for pulling away, he cranked the ignition. "The first thing we'll do when we hit town is have a doctor take a look at that cut and your nose."

"That's not necessary."

"It's what I want to do, so humor me."

"I'd rather not waste the time."

"Too bad."

She crossed her arms. "Argh. I hate how bossy you are."

"You better get used to it. I'm not likely to change real soon." He instantly regretted his rude behavior, but the way she pulled away from him as if he had the plague when all he wanted to do was tunnel his fingers into her hair and kiss her made him mad. And that made him even madder.

Why was he getting mad over a little thing like her not wanting him to touch her when the last thing he wanted was a relationship? Especially not a relationship with a woman who'd already proved when push came to shove she'd act just like Lori, running into the line of fire to save others. He couldn't live with that hanging over his head. It didn't end well. Most of the time it ended catastrophically. He'd already experienced enough tragedy in his life that he wasn't foolish enough to go looking for more.

If only he could remember that the next time he looked into Kat's eyes and all of his resolve melted away.

FIVE

Kat held the ice pack on her nose that the urgent care doctor had given her and stared out the car window. The sun had set while he poked and prodded her face, and the darkness added to her grumpy mood. And so did Mitch's lack of apology for going all caveman on her, thumping his chest and telling her what to do like her dad had done with her mom.

If he'd listened to her at all when she'd told him about her issue with men trying to take charge on the job, he would surely have apologized. Either he didn't think he'd been rude or he didn't really listen to her before. Both options left her irritated.

She studied him, all dark and brooding in the dim lighting as he concentrated on easing through heavy traffic. They were on their way to his place. His decision, of course. Everything had to be by his rules. She got that they couldn't go to the office because she shouldn't be helping with this case, but they could meet Tommy elsewhere.

She'd object, but what could she say? She couldn't tell him she didn't need to see where he lived—see his things, his life—and think about him as a person instead of a fellow investigator. She'd had enough personal contact when he'd held and protected her earlier. Now, even despite his failure to apologize, she still wanted more and that just couldn't happen.

He glanced at her and caught her staring. She didn't look away.

"Your nose broken?" Those were the first words he'd spoken since dropping her off at the clinic.

"No."

"That's good then."

"Yeah."

"And the cut didn't need stitches I see."

She lowered the ice to see him better. "This your way of saying you're sorry for being so bossy earlier?"

"Kind of."

She watched him and waited for him to go on.

"Look," he said, clicking on the blinker, "I *am* sorry for getting mad and being a jerk. But—and I hope you'll remember this—I'll never apologize for doing what I think is best for you."

"And why will I need to remember that?"

He turned onto a street in an older Portland neighborhood undergoing revitalization. "Something tells me we're going to have this discussion again before the day is over."

"Could you be any more cryptic?"

He laughed. "I could try."

She was still miffed at him, but she couldn't help but smile at his sudden good mood so she looked out the window to hide it.

His phone rang from a dashboard holder.

"Hello," Mitch answered.

"Mitchy, it's me." A pitiful woman's voice came over the speaker. "How are you?"

"Angie?"

"Yeah. Don't you know your own sister's voice anymore?"

"It's been a long time." His voice held that iron tone of earlier. "What do you want?"

"I just wanted to see how you are."

"If you're calling, Angie, you want something. What is it?"

"Why are you being so mean?" She started crying.

He sighed and Kat could see the raw pain on his face. "I'm not trying to be mean, honey. I just can't enable your addiction anymore. You know that."

"Fine." Silence followed.

"Angie?" he asked. "Angie?" He waited. "Great. Hang up on me." He tapped the end button and glanced at Kat. "My sister. Angie. Homeless drug addict." He said it so matter-of-factly that it broke Kat's heart. If she didn't see the genuine distress on his face, she would think he was an uncaring man.

"Is there anything I can do?"

"The only thing Angie needs is rehab and she refuses to go." He sounded so defeated. So hurt. And so closed.

He pulled into the narrow driveway of a small home and killed the engine. The light mounted by the back door gave off a warming glow and highlighted Tommy's Jeep sitting at the back of the drive.

Kat eased out of the car but Mitch didn't follow. She looked back. He sat with his forehead on the steering wheel. She knew this kind of pain. The kind brought on by someone you love slowly killing themself. She ought to know, she'd cried herself to sleep too many nights to count after seeing the same thing in her dad. The only difference was he took her mom with him to the grave.

She went around the car and opened Mitch's door. "What can I do?"

He lifted his head and shook it before climbing out. As the misery in his gaze washed over her, she didn't think twice, but slipped her arms around him and hugged. He was solid and strong, yet now she knew how vulnerable he was, too, so she offered a silent prayer for him and Angie.

Mitch settled his chin on her head and tightened the strong arms circling her. The warmth of his body and the even thumping of his chest kept the chilly air at bay. She felt safe.

Like when her brothers hugged her, but there was more. A deep yearning to know everything about this man. To take a chance. To go beyond the superficial and find out what kind of person he really was.

She leaned back and looked up at him. He wasn't just a good-looking man. He was deep and caring. Loving...when he let himself be.

He lifted his hand and ran it gently over her hair, before letting it slide down her arm to twine with her fingers. "You're getting wet. We should go inside." He smiled softly and gave a gentle tug.

She didn't want the moment to pass, but it was dangerous to her heart to stay like this so she let him pull her through the drizzle into a small kitchen in disarray. He dropped her hand and she stopped to catch her breath from running—maybe from the way she'd responded to the hug—to look around the room.

Cabinet doors were missing and rough plywood served as his countertop. The wood floor was a checkerboard of patches and tools were discarded as if left where he'd last used them.

"I'm remodeling," he said and kept walking. "Watch your step." He slipped through a wall of thick plastic hanging from the ceiling. He didn't seem the least bit aware of her emotions. A good thing. Right?

On the other side of the makeshift wall, a dog barked excitedly and jumped up to greet Mitch as he held the plastic aside for her.

"About time," she heard Tommy say.

She carefully stepped over a hole running the length of the room where a wall had obviously once stood.

Before she could get a good look at the room, Tommy walked up to her and lifted her chin. "Nice shiner, Justice."

"I could give you a matching one, if you want."

He laughed then pulled her in for a hug. "Glad to see you're alive and kicking, partner."

"Glad to be alive," she replied and was surprised how the reference to her as his partner put a tremor in her voice.

"If you two are done making nice. we have work to do," Mitch muttered.

"What's wrong with him?" Tommy let her go and stepped back.

"You'll have to ask him. He's been a grump all afternoon." She tried to sound lighthearted when she knew he really was upset about his sister.

"That true, Elliot?"

"Work. We have work to do." He went to the far end of the great room where he straddled a chair by a contemporary teak table. His dog trotted after him. Kat couldn't identify a breed. Most likely a pound puppy.

She slowly followed, admiring Mitch's taste in furnishings. She'd expected the usual black leather and massive TV typical of bachelors, but found a tailored sectional in a dark brown and a modest-size flat screen on the wall above a glass-tiled fireplace surround.

Tommy dropped a folder on the table and took a seat at the far end. She slipped into a chair between the two of them and the dog came over to sniff her.

"What's your dog's name?" she asked.

Tommy started laughing. "Her name is Princess. A cop with a dog named Princess. I can just see the look on a date's face if he ever brought one home and introduced them."

"She had that name when I adopted her from the shelter." Mitch's tone was low but held no warning.

"I think it's sweet." She ruffled Princess's ears.

"Yeah, you're such a bleeding heart, you would." Tommy laughed.

"One of us had to have compassion on the job." She wrinkled her nose at her partner. Former partner, she reminded herself. The tough as nails, self-made man was with Mitch now. Mitch was now the kinder, gentler person on the team. She'd seen his heart. His caring. A stark contrast to Tommy's abrasive personality. They made a good team just as she and Tommy had.

"So bring us up to speed," Mitch commanded in his usual forthright tone, moving them back to their reason for being there.

Tommy didn't seem to balk at Mitch's bossiness but looked at her. "I put a rush on the DNA from your fingernail scrapings, but with the way things are always backlogged at O.S.P. a rush could still take days to process." The Oregon State Police Crime Lab was constrained by budget restrictions so they had to triage requests. "I also included a cigarette butt found near the van and there were several good fingerprints lifted at Nancy Bodig's house."

"Not likely our killer's, though," Kat said as Princess circled and lay down by her feet. "He wore gloves."

"Were any prints from unknown individuals?" Mitch asked.

"There were two good latents that didn't belong to Kat, Nancy or Nathan Bodig. We ran those through A.F.I.S. No hits." The Automated Fingerprint Identification System database held prints for convicted felons and civil servants.

"So our forensic evidence is limited to the DNA, two prints, the paint transfer and a few digits of a license plate," Kat recapped.

Mitch turned to Tommy. "Tell me you have something else for us 'cause that's not a whole lot to go on."

"I spent the day tracking down illegal sources for propofol. Thankfully the network for black market pharmaceuticals isn't as large as recreational drugs."

"So you have some promising leads, then?" Kat asked.

Tommy nodded. "I'll run them down tomorrow."

The doorbell rang and Princess popped up, but didn't bark.

"I ordered Chinese." Tommy didn't move to answer the door.

"Let me guess," Mitch said, standing. "Since we're at my house, I'm buying."

"Well, if you're offering, go for it." Tommy laughed and tugged Kat to her feet. "C'mon, Justice. Help me get plates and silverware from the hole in the wall he calls a kitchen." He crossed the room and stopped at the plastic wall. "Hold this open so I don't contaminate things with drywall dust."

She grabbed the plastic, feeling the gritty residue linger on her fingers. "Mitch told me Nancy's parents met you at the morgue this morning."

"Sad thing losing both their kids like that." He retrieved plates from an airtight storage container on the counter.

"I'd like to talk to them. Can I get their contact info?"

"I'll email it to you." He dug out silverware and piled it on top of the plates.

She heard the front door close and the rich aroma of spices trailed Mitch into the dining room, making her stomach rumble.

"Man, Justice." Tommy looked at her as he grabbed sodas from the refrigerator. "Didn't he feed you today?"

"We didn't have time."

"There's always time to eat."

"We had that little incident that kept us busy. Then we went to the salvage yard and after that, Mitch insisted I see a doctor about my nose."

"And you went?"

"Yeah."

He grabbed the plates and stared at her. "You, Kat Justice, went to see a doctor for a bump on the nose?"

"Mitch didn't take no for an answer."

His eyebrows shot up. "Well, well, well."

"What's that supposed to mean?"

He balanced everything in his hands and headed her way. "It means that my little Kitty Kat is still interested in Mitch Elliot."

"What? Where'd you get that idea? I only did it because he'd have sat there staring at me until I went in."

"Uh-huh, keep telling yourself that, Kat." He walked past her, and she turned to see Mitch staring at them.

His smug little smile said he'd clearly heard the conversation. Okay, so maybe it wasn't smug, but soft and adorable and almost irresistible, compelling her to return it with one of her own. His smile spread and if she was right, she saw in his eyes everything she'd hoped to see when she'd confessed her crush. Interest. Big, bold and unsettling.

She wasn't going there. Couldn't go there with a man who proved his penchant for being in charge just like her dad. She forcibly dragged her gaze away and followed Tommy back to the dining room. She'd resist Mitch Elliot now and she could only hope she'd find the resolve to resist him later and forget all about the way that lopsided grin made her heart beat faster.

After they finished eating, Mitch sat back to watch Kat hash out investigative details with Tommy. Between bites of Kung Pao chicken, he'd brought them up to speed on Nancy's background check. An accountant, she'd worked from home with a long and dedicated client list, and she appeared to have been an upright citizen in every way.

Not that Mitch actually caught all of the details. Instead, he kept replaying the conversation he'd overheard in the kitchen. He couldn't stop wondering if Tommy was right when he'd said Kat was still interested in him. He couldn't see how agreeing to go to a doctor in any way indicated her interest.

But Tommy knew her better than anyone could, and he'd said that was what it meant.

Like any of it mattered. Nothing had changed. He may still want to go out with her as he had back in her rookie days and it was flattering that she might return the feelings, but he wouldn't do anything about it.

Unless of course he could guarantee that something bad wouldn't happen to her. But that wasn't something anyone but God could guarantee and despite Kat's insistence that God was watching over them, Mitch still wasn't certain.

"You want to weigh in on this one, Elliot, or are you gonna stare at Kat all night?" Tommy asked before giving him a wry smile.

Mitch thought to deny that he was staring but he'd been caught red-handed. "Weigh in on what?"

"We were discussing how Nancy checks out clean as a whistle. And I said she seems to be a dead end and we should keep working the brother angle. Like seeing if any of his clients or coworkers held a grudge."

"I agree we should keep after the brother's so-called accident, but I also think we should investigate Nancy's clients, too. As an accountant, she would have access to a lot of money and there's no better motive for murder than money. Plus no one is as clean as you say Nancy is."

"Like I said, man, she was a regular saint. Her finances are stellar. Wish mine were half as good. She spent all her free time volunteering at her church and a homeless shelter. Her neighbors idolized her. What's to find?"

"He's right, Mitch," Kat added. "Everyone loved Nancy. She was the sweetest, kindest woman, and she didn't deserve this."

"Maybe she *is* clean," Mitch conceded. "But that doesn't mean her clients are. We can't stop until we work every angle. That includes talking to her clients. And we need to go through her things and her brother's if we can locate his stuff."

"Nancy told me her parents couldn't bear to deal with his things so she had them all moved to her attic," Kat offered.

"So first thing tomorrow I'll start on the list of clients and you two can interview Bodig's boss." Tommy flipped his notebook closed. "Then we'll all meet up and go through her house."

"I'll work with you, Tommy," Kat said.

Mitch could tell she was trying to sound laid back about this as if she thought spending another day with him didn't matter, but she failed to carry it off. He opened his mouth to argue, but closed it before he said something he'd regret. Being with her wasn't a good idea on a personal level for either of them, but he couldn't help but get miffed each time she tried to avoid him.

"Since you know Bodig's case so well, it's better if you go with Mitch." Tommy looked at Kat, his expression confrontational, very reminiscent of how he treated uncooperative suspects.

The nonverbal sparring between the old partners continued, and Mitch sat back to watch. Tommy could tell Kat didn't want to do this and yet he was pushing her. But Tommy was a worthy opponent. Mitch had lost plenty of battles with his stubborn partner.

Still, her eyes fought back as she crossed her arms. "Mitch could interview the clients and you could come with me to see Nathan's boss."

"We'll leave it like it is," Tommy said, his eyes never leaving Kat. "It'd take too much time to bring each other up to speed to change now."

"I agree," Mitch added, and Kat faced him. "Two to one, Kat. You're outvoted."

She looked disappointed for a few moments, but then she

gave a clipped nod and glanced at her watch. "So if this is settled I'd like to get going. Can you give me a ride, Tommy?"

"I'm not letting you go home tonight." Mitch's words flew out, and he saw her visibly recoil.

"That's not really your decision to make, Mitch." Her tone was soft, but there was a hint of warning hidden in its depths.

So what? After the shooting this afternoon, he wouldn't back down. "You can stay with someone in your family or here with me. Your choice."

She swung her gaze to Tommy, her eyes pleading. "Tommy'll let me crash on his couch, won't you Tommy?"

"Ah, sorry, Kat, but you know my little brother's staying with me right now and my place isn't even big enough for one person."

Kat got up, her eyes never leaving Tommy. "Can I have a word with you in the other room?"

He rose and followed her. Mitch wanted to go after them to make sure Tommy didn't cave and let her go home alone, but the last thing Mitch wanted to hear her say right now was that she'd rather face a killer than spend time with him.

Kat stormed into the kitchen, fighting her frustration at Tommy for siding with Mitch. Why did Mitch think he could decide these things for her? And Tommy. He was supposed to be on her side. Have her back. Sure, Mitch was his current partner, but she'd sat beside this man for five years. Five years, for goodness' sake. That had to count for something.

She stopped next to the sink. "Why are you doing this?"

"Doing what, Kat?" His tone was innocent, making her madder.

"You know I can't stay here."

"Why not?" More innocent.

"Don't play dumb with me Tommy Flannigan. You know what I mean."

"Can't say it, huh?" He grinned.

"Ooh, you make me so mad sometimes." She fisted her hands.

He came closer and looked down on her. "Listen, Kitty Kat. Mitch is one of the good guys. I oughta know. I spend most of my day with him. He's into you, and I'm not going to help you run away and hide from him."

"I'm not running away. I just don't want to be alone with him."

"Then don't. Go stay with someone in your family."

"You know that's not an option for me."

"I get that you want to keep them safe, Kat, but they're bound to get involved in this sooner or later."

"Dani's promised to hold them off as long as possible, and I hope to have this resolved before they try to intervene."

"Then you'll have to decide if you're more afraid of someone you already love getting hurt or risk staying here, finding out that Mitch isn't a bad guy and the two of you could be great together. Either way, Kat, it's up to you." He slung an arm around her shoulder and gave her a brotherly hug. "But I agree with Mitch. You won't be going home tonight."

There had to be a compromise. Something she could do to put a buffer between her and Mitch and yet not threaten anyone's safety.

She looked up at him. "You could stay here with us."

He erupted in a belly laugh. "You don't think I'd make it that easy on you, do you?" He squeezed her shoulders, then released her. "I'll see you tomorrow."

Feeling betrayed by her best friend, she watched him walk away. She heard him talking with Mitch then the door open and close. She couldn't hide out in the kitchen all night, but she didn't want to face Mitch. Tommy said he was into her. Part of her was thrilled. The other part was terrified.

Mitch lifted the plastic, that charming smile on his face

again. "My guest room is more comfortable than spending the night in here."

Her mind flew over the possibilities of what to do. Maybe someone else could stay here with them and run interference. She could call Dani. Their killer didn't know that Kat was here so Dani would be safe here, too. Kat would have to put up with her sister's meddling and asking a lot of questions about Mitch, but she wouldn't try to push Kat into something the way Tommy was doing.

"Kat?" Mitch asked, uncertainty clouding his usually bright eyes.

Eyes that were intriguing and compelling her to move closer. She took a step back instead. "I'd like to call my sister, Dani, and have her drop off some things for me."

He let out a breath as if he'd been holding it in anticipation of her answer. "Of course."

"Oh, and by the way, Mitch. She'll be spending the night here, too." Kat slipped through the opening to get her phone from the dining room table. She didn't hear him follow, so she stopped and looked back.

His eyes never left her, and he stood there strong and solid with a hint of vulnerability that she'd seen earlier and made her heart beat faster.

She had to admit he was the whole package. Tall, dark and handsome as well as kind and generous. Fortunately for her he was also bossy and domineering, and right now that was the only thing keeping her from crossing the room and getting lost in those captivating eyes.

SIX

The next morning, Kat and Dani sat at Mitch's small breakfast area table while Mitch watched them over a cup of steaming coffee. The sisters were sharing their morning devotions and Kat kept trying to include him in the discussion about why bad things happen to good people.

Surprisingly, he'd almost caved and bought into the idea that God's plan was perfect, but the angry, purple bruise on Kat's face kept reminding him of how hard it was to believe that.

Still, it had been nice to watch the sisters interact. Since they weren't blood relatives they didn't look anything alike, but their mannerisms and movements were similar. Both were sparse with their words and neither of them used their hands when talking.

Dani was a gorgeous blonde, the kind of perfect-looking woman found in magazines, but it was Kat who kept drawing his attention. And yet he had to focus on everything but her to keep from scaring her with the intensity of his interest. Maybe scaring himself.

Dani closed her Bible and slid effortlessly to her feet, clad in three-inch heels. "I need to get to the office before Cole comes looking for me."

Kat rose, too. Her boot heels equally as high didn't bring

her anywhere near Dani's height. "Make sure you tell every-one the investigation into Nancy's death is going well."

Dani raised an eyebrow, her expression clearly amused. "Translated, don't tell them how freaked out you still are about this or they'll come running."

"That's not what I said." Kat planted a hand on her hip. She was adorable when she tried to be so tough. The little bit of a woman looked like a little puppy ready to fight a big wolf.

Dani turned to him. "It was good to meet you, Mitch. And thanks for taking care of Kat."

Kat shot a look at her sister's back that said she didn't need Mitch to take care of her. "I'll walk you to the door."

They left the room and Mitch cleaned up the mess from breakfast. After a call from Tommy informing him that the lab found no obvious sign of tampering with Bodig's car other than the paint residue, and then arranging a meeting with Bodig's boss, Mitch had run out to a local bagel place and offered the meager fare on paper plates. He wished his house wasn't such a mess or he could've cooked them a hot meal before going out into the unusually cold, bleak day.

At least he didn't have to compromise on the coffee. He kept a supply of fresh roasted Guatemalan beans on hand at all times. He grabbed a couple of travel mugs and split the remainder of the pot between them.

Kat came back into the room. "What time is our appoint-ment with Weichert?"

"Nine-thirty." He handed her one of the travel mugs and smiled as he remembered how cute she looked a few minutes ago when she got upset with Dani.

She took the cup. "I really need this. You must be able to read my mind."

"Not hardly, but I wish I could."

Her smile disappeared, replaced with a frown.

He wanted to ask what put that frown on her face, but

honestly, he was afraid to hear the answer so he found an ice pack in the refrigerator, wrapped it in a towel and held it out. "For your nose."

"Thanks for thinking of this," she said softly with no hint of residual anger for not letting her go home last night.

"We should be going." He grabbed his jacket from a peg and stepped outside. It was cold enough to snow, but the forecast was calling for clear skies. Still a hazy fog hung over the area and he couldn't see much past the end of his driveway as he settled Kat into the car.

"Tommy and I were talking about Bodig's girlfriend, Olivia, this morning," he said once he'd navigated the heaviest of traffic through the city. "Maybe you could tell me why you ruled her out."

"For starters, she had an airtight alibi. She didn't leave her apartment all night and her roommate was with her."

"Any likelihood this roommate would lie for her?"

"Maybe but the alibi was corroborated by the apartment manager. He said Olivia's and the roommate's cars were both there at the time of the crash."

He glanced at her. "Kind of odd for an apartment manager to know something like that, don't you think?"

"Not in this case. He'd arranged to have a vehicle towed from a private parking space adjacent to Olivia's space, and he was sitting outside waiting for the tow company."

She peered at him as if she thought he might question what she said, but when he didn't she continued. "She also gave us full access to her computer, cell phone and bank account. Dani's a computer expert and she inspected all of it. We found no motive for why Olivia would want Nathan dead."

"I have to admit if she got cold feet and wanted to back out of the wedding that it's a little extreme to kill him."

"I don't know, it works for me."

He shot her a shocked look and she laughed, a full, throaty

laugh that he'd never heard before. Amazing, beautiful, and he wanted to find a way to repeat it. But they arrived at the brightly painted field office for the Oregon Department of Human Services, and they wouldn't be laughing again for a while anyway.

He found a parking spot and directed Kat to the reception desk in the lobby where he held his shield out. "Detective Elliot. We have an appointment with Mr. Weichert."

The older woman took one look at his badge and flinched. Not an unusual reaction from someone after they realized a cop had come to question someone they knew.

"He's expecting you," she said, her fingers already flying over buttons on her phone. "I'll page him."

She didn't tell them to sit so he leaned back on the desk and watched the door. Kat focused in the same direction, and he noticed that the ice pack had brought down the swelling of her nose.

The door opened and Kat pulled her shoulders back. Ready for battle. At least she seemed to think this was going to be a battle. Mitch didn't think the guy had anything to hide.

"Detective Elliot." The thin man with a severely receding hairline stuck out a bony hand. "Robert Weichert."

Mitch wasn't surprised at Weichert's wimpy handshake. He figured a slight wind would blow him over. "This is Katherine Justice." Mitch nodded at Kat.

Weichert shook her hand. "Please follow me."

He swiped a keycard and they went down a dimly lit hallway to a small office without windows. Files were piled high on a credenza, but the desk was neat and tidy. Weichert sat behind the desk and started drumming his fingers on top.

Kat gave him a hard look and Mitch recognized it as her way of telling Weichert that they were in charge of this interview. Cops did this all the time to set the stage.

"What can you tell me about Nathan Bodig, Mr. Weichert?"

Mitch settled onto a hard chair and felt the stab of pain from one of the many bruises he'd sustained yesterday.

"He was such a good man. Dedicated. Hard-working. As close to an ideal employee as they come." Weichert shook his head. "We're all still just shocked over his accident."

"Actually that's what we wanted to talk about, Mr. Weichert," Mitch said. "We're beginning to question if it really was an accident."

Weichert sat forward. "You mean you think someone may have caused the crash on purpose?"

"It's possible. Can you think of anyone who might've wanted to harm Mr. Bodig?"

Weichert's eyes opened wide. "No. No, of course not. Everyone around here liked him."

"What about his clients?" Kat asked. "Was there someone who might've been upset with him?"

"What we do often impacts lives in what our clients think are adverse ways. They get angry with us all the time and some even take it a step further and make threats. But there were no credible threats made against Nathan."

"When you say 'credible,' what does that mean exactly?" Kat ended with a raised brow.

"We investigate every threat we receive. You can never be too careful, is my motto. But our investigations never turned up anything more than clients and their families blowing off steam."

"Do you keep these threats on file?" Mitch asked.

"Yes. Each of us is instructed to keep such a file."

"Can we look at Mr. Bodig's file?" Kat's hard look said it wasn't optional.

"Now that you mention it, I don't remember my assistant asking me what to do with that file when she cleaned out Nathan's cubicle. Let me check with her." He picked up the phone and dialed. "Margaret, did you find a threat file in

Nathan's belongings?" He listened, his finger resting on the side of his narrow face. "Okay, thank you." He put down the phone. "She didn't find one, but Nathan was a by-the-book kind of guy so I'm sure he kept a file."

"So where is it, then?" Kat asked, sounding as if she thought Weichert was lying.

"That's a good question."

"Could someone else in your office have taken it?" Mitch asked before Kat completely took over the interview.

"Why would they want to do that?"

"Maybe to cover up something." Kat leaned closer and watched him intently.

"Like what?" Weichert's eyes narrowed. "We have nothing to hide here."

"We don't think you do," Mitch jumped in as he gave Kat a look, telling her to chill. "You're sure there's no one in the office that might have a grudge against Mr. Bodig?"

"I'm positive, Detective." He sighed. "This is a stressful job, and I work hard to foster teamwork. If someone had it in for Nathan I'd know about it."

"We'd still like the name and contact information for all of his coworkers. And the same information for his clients for the last ninety days."

Weichert's back went up. "You know I can't do that, Detective. All of our information is confidential, and I can't just hand it over. But if you'd get a court order, I'd be happy to oblige."

Legally what the man had said was true, but officials in Weichert's position often cooperated in investigations. Maybe Mitch could persuade him with a little push. "I have no problem getting that order, but if you make me do that, I'll think you're hiding something." He turned to Kat. "What do we do when someone's hiding things?"

"We start digging. Maybe tail the person. Wait for the

least little mistake to haul them in." She smiled at Weichert. "You wouldn't want us to do that would you, Mr. Weichert?"

"That's not fair."

"Neither is the fact that Nathan Bodig may have been murdered," Mitch said. "Either you want to help us find the killer or you don't."

"It's not that I don't want to help, but I'll lose my job if I turn over confidential files."

"Tell you what, Weichert." Mitch leaned forward. "At least give me the information on the clients right now, and I'll get to work on that court order to show the higher-ups in case anyone asks."

"You're not just trying to play me, are you?"

"He's a man of his word," Kat added with respect and admiration in her eyes that made Mitch's heart warm.

Weichert seemed to mull it over, then turned to his keyboard and started clicking away. As Mitch shared a victory smile with Kat the printer whirred behind Weichert and started spitting out pages.

"Here you go," Weichert said tersely as he grabbed the pages. "Now if you don't mind I have work to do."

Mitch rose, towering over the guy, who shrank back. "I'd also appreciate it if you'd ask around to see if anyone else might know what happened to Mr. Bodig's threat file."

"I will."

"Call me if you find anything." Mitch gave him his business card.

"You won't forget about the order?" Weichert's confidence had all but evaporated.

"I said I'd do it, Mr. Weichert, and that means I'll do it." Mitch waited for Kat to exit the room then he followed.

In the hallway, she let out a long breath. "So exactly how are you planning to get that court order without any solid evidence to back it up?"

"I'm hoping we'll come up with something that I can use by the end of the day." Mitch met her gaze.

"And if we don't?"

"I didn't actually promise to get one, just said I'd try to get one. And I will try." They went through the lobby, and he held open the front door. "Nancy's place to search Bodig's things?"

"You read my mind," she answered and they stepped into the cool morning with the sun trying to break free.

They made their way to the car and Mitch settled in for the task of navigating traffic. He loved living in Portland, but he could live without the heavy traffic.

"You think Weichert was hiding something?" Kat asked when he turned into Nancy's neighborhood.

"Not really, do you?"

"No. He seemed like a straight shooter until we asked for the records." She seemed confident in her opinion. "He wouldn't be the first official who followed rules and made us get a court order."

"It is odd that Bodig's threat file is missing, though."

"Let's hope we find it at Nancy's."

He clicked on a blinker and turned onto Nancy's street. "If she had the file, wouldn't she have given it to you when you started looking into his death?"

"If it's there, I doubt she even knew she had it. She was just like her parents. She could never bring herself to go through his stuff. I was supposed to go through it, but I was tied up on another case. Maybe if I'd gotten to it sooner—" Kat bit her lip and looked away.

"Hey," he said as he pulled into Nancy's driveway. "I thought you were over blaming yourself for all of this."

"I'm trying, but after I made my condolence call to Nancy's parents last night it all came back. I keep thinking if I'd just done something different Nancy would still be alive." The confident woman of a few moments ago vanished.

He rested his hand on hers. "Don't go there, Kat, okay? Remember what you told me, God has a plan here."

"You don't really believe that."

"But you do. And I'm trying to."

She smiled. "I'm happy to hear that."

"I thought you might be." He squeezed her hand.

The sun slipped free of morning clouds, the warmth shining through the windshield as if it'd come out just to encourage her to cheer up. Mitch made a quick visual assessment of the area. Other than an official seal on the door, you'd never know a murder had taken place in this sleepy neighborhood.

"Looks clear," he said as his phone rang. "That's Tommy's ring tone. Hopefully he has some news for us," Mitch said but Kat had already climbed out and started up the walk.

He grabbed the phone and by the time he got out, she was on the stairs leading to the porch. That was Kat. Always in a hurry. But she'd have to wait for him to break the seal Tommy had placed on the door.

He punched talk. "What's up, Tommy?"

Crack.

A bullet whizzed past Mitch and splintered the front door. Kat whirled around, her eyes wide.

"Get down!" he yelled as he drew his weapon, took cover behind the car door and searched for the shooter in one swift move. He swept his gaze right, left, front, back. Saw no one. He turned back to Kat and it was as if everything in front of him changed to slow motion. She pivoted and dived slowly toward the porch, taking him back to another time. Another place. Lori, with a bullet in her chest, blood spurting, dropping to the ground, her eyes open. Staring vacant.

"What's going on?" Tommy's voice came from his phone.

"We have a shooter. Send backup."

Crack.

Another bullet.

Kat, still trying to take cover, jerked, then landed on the porch with a loud thud.

She'd been hit.

Mitch's heart skipped a beat. He wanted to race up the walk and throw himself over her, but he couldn't help her if he was shot, too.

Another bullet whizzed over her head and into the door.

She lay there unmoving. Not even a flinch. She was hit all right, and despite everything he'd been trained to do, he couldn't just sit here. He made his way to the front of his car, then to the garage. He waited a few seconds. No more gunfire. He bolted to his feet and charged up the walkway where he spotted blood pooling under her.

"Kat," he yelled and charged faster. He scooped her up in his arms, then dove behind shrubbery blocking the shooter's view of the porch. He landed on his shoulder to shield her from the impact then rolled to cover her body.

"Ouch," she said, and his heart soared. She was alive.

He lay there, waiting to hear another gunshot over the thudding of his heart or maybe the pounding of footsteps as the shooter came to finish them off. He tightened the arm hooked around her waist and lifted his head from where he'd buried it in her hair. "Where are you hit?"

"He just grazed my arm," she said as if she'd just fallen down and skinned her knee not taken a bullet in the arm.

He rolled off her, and she looked at him, her face inches from his. "You might've warned me you were going to go all he-man on me again." She frowned at him.

Relief flooded through his chest. He wanted to pull her to him and hold her, but settled for smoothing her hair out of her face and looking at her.

"What?" she asked.

"You shouldn't have just laid there in the line of fire, Kat."

"I knew I couldn't take cover faster than he could fire.

I hoped he'd think I was down so he'd stop firing. In case you didn't notice it seemed to work." She gave a little smile. "What about you? Are you hit?"

"No."

"God came through again." She gave a tremulous smile.

He smiled back at her and cupped the side of her face. She was right, of course. God had kept them both alive. But that didn't take away the feeling in the pit of his stomach. He'd only felt this helpless once. With Lori on the day she died. And he never wanted to feel it again. "Promise me you'll stay by my side from now on. When I go, you go. When I stop, you stop."

He saw a brief flicker of fear in her eyes. So she *was* scared, but putting on a good show. This time he didn't resist but drew her into his arms. She smeiled fresh and sweet and he hated that she'd been hit. Hated the rise of all of the doubts brought on by lingering guilt over Lori's death.

"Promise me, Kat," he whispered into her hair, his plea so urgent it scared him.

"I'll stay by your side."

He heard her words, felt the sincerity in them, but how could he relax when a killer still stalked her?

SEVEN

Kat sat on the back of the ambulance, her arm aching far worse than she'd let on to Mitch. Sweet, caring Mitch. Strong Mitch, holding her against that solid wall of his chest again. Stroking her back and making her feel safe.

What was she going to do about that man? She wanted to dislike him. To not respect him. But the more time she spent with him, the more she saw he was just what Tommy said last night. A good guy. A good guy who just happened to look amazing. Behind the handsome face and toned body that her medic kept checking out, was a man she could fall hopelessly in love with if she weren't careful.

She sighed and dropped her chin to her chest to loosen cramping muscles in her neck.

What am I going to do here, Lord? You saved us both. Kept us from harm. But it feels like You're just pushing me into more trouble by keeping Mitch near me. You know I can't handle a relationship. I need Your help, Father. Don't let me do something I'll regret.

"Hey, partner." Tommy's voice brought her head up. He squatted in front of her and took her hands. "I hear you're refusing to go to the hospital."

"I'll go, just not in the ambulance."

"That's what I figured you'd say so Mitch is going to drive you while I go through Bodig's files."

"No! Please. You can take me."

"I can't."

"Why on earth not?" She felt anger taking over.

"Because Mitch is letting this get to him, and he needs to be with you to get over it."

She watched Tommy like a hawk trying to gage his sincerity. His eyes were clear, honest and transparent, but that didn't mean anything. "Is this just a ploy to get me in the car with him or are you serious about helping Mitch?"

He scrunched his eyes. "Mitch may not have told you, but he lost a partner in a situation very much like this one."

"He mentioned it."

"So you can imagine how this has upset him. He's over there acting like it doesn't bother him, but it doesn't take a rocket scientist to see he's stressed."

She looked at Mitch standing near the house talking on the phone with his hand clamped on the back of his neck. His posture was rigid and his jaw tight. She remembered when he'd said he worried about this exact thing happening and not being able to stop it. Of course he was talking about someone he cared about then. Not her. So Tommy was way off base here.

She moved her focus back to Tommy. "I don't get how taking me to the hospital is going to help with that."

"On the ride over, you can convince him that this wasn't his fault, and he'll get a chance to see that you really are okay."

Was Tommy really being honest with her, or was he just trying to play matchmaker?

"So this is really about Mitch and not you meddling in our lives?"

"Okay, fine. Maybe I'm meddling a little." He shifted and

leaned closer. "But this is the first time I've ever seen you let your guard down around any guy, and I'm not going to stand around and watch you let it pass by without doing something about it."

She studied him again. Her partner. Former partner. Mr. Macho. Squatting there and giving her advice on her love life. It suddenly hit her as hilarious and she started laughing. She saw Mitch's eyebrow raise in question, then his eyes cloud with concern. He probably thought she was going into shock and losing it. She was losing it all right, but not from shock.

"What?" Tommy asked, clearly baffled by her behavior.

She shook her head. "You. The man who has never had a relationship longer than a month giving me advice."

He smiled, an adorable grin that women had a hard time ignoring. "I do all right with the ladies."

"I know you do, but trust me, that does not qualify you to give relationship advice." She stood, felt a little lightheaded and wobbled. Tommy shot out an arm to steady her, and Mitch came rushing over.

She took a step back and planted a hand on the side of the ambulance. She appreciated Tommy's and Mitch's concern, but she didn't appreciate their continued coddling in front of the other law enforcement personnel swarming the scene.

Intent on giving him a warning look she peered up at Mitch, but the warm concern was alive and glowing in his eyes and she felt all of her reserve melt away in the heat. She was so in over her head here. She'd just been shot by a killer and right now this look Mitch had trained on her felt far more dangerous than the man threatening her life.

In the hospital waiting room, Mitch laid his head back against the cushioned chair, closed his eyes and replayed their ride to the E.R. Something had changed between them on the ride over here. Or at least something changed with Kat. She was more cheerful and positive. Making sure he knew she was fine and treating him as if she felt like he needed cheering up. Who knows, maybe Tommy said something in their little discussion to make her change.

Not that it mattered. Mitch had just guaranteed her mood was about to crash. He'd done the unthinkable. The minute the medics arrived and took over Kat's care, he'd ignored wishes that she'd made completely and totally known to him, and he'd phoned her family. Now he had to figure out how to tell her that Cole—once he got over yelling at Mitch for not involving him sooner—had agreed to meet them at her house and work alongside Mitch to keep her safe.

He could already see her reaction. She'd fist her petite hands, plant them on her hips, maybe jut her jaw out like she did sometimes and let him have it verbally. That he wouldn't mind so much as she'd get over it. But he also knew there'd be a healthy measure of disappointment and pain of betrayal in her eyes for going behind her back.

The worst part was that he understood her reason for keeping her family out of this. Distance protected people. He lived by that motto and let it control him and keep him from getting too close. Still, despite the need to protect himself, he cared. No matter how much he fought it, he cared. About Angie, Tommy and now Kat. More than he wanted to admit.

Just like his mom always hoped he would. She'd begged him to let go of his worry and live again. Quoting the Bible to him, and reminding him that worrying can't add a single hour to his life. So give it up, she'd said. He'd tried and succeeded for a while, but then she'd died, bringing all of his worries to fruition, and he'd chalked up that piece of advice as meaningless. But he was starting to think he'd been wrong. At least Kat was making him reconsider his stance.

A hand touched the shoulder he'd slid across the porch on, and a searing pain shot down his arm. He knew it had to be Kat, but he didn't want her to know how bad his shoulder hurt so he took a few deep breaths to keep the pain at bay before opening his eyes.

"Trying to catch a quick nap?" She smiled down on him and no matter his recent thoughts, no matter his dread at telling her what he'd done, he smiled back, taking a few moments just to enjoy her good mood before he dropped his bomb.

"Everything okay?" he finally asked.

She lifted her arm with a cut-off shirtsleeve and a bandage circling her bicep. "I'm good to go."

"Then let's get out of here." He got up and led the way to the door. She tried to slip into her jacket and fumbled. He grabbed the back and helped her shrug into it. Then, instead of walking away as he should do, he freed her hair and let it settle over her shoulders, the silky strands curling around his fingers.

"Thanks," she said and looked up at him again, her gaze was as soft as a caress. "I seem to be thanking you a lot lately."

"No thanks needed." His eyes clung to hers, not wanting to break away, but he forced himself to pull free. "Wait here. I'll go get the car."

He rushed outside and jogged to his car, letting the cold air wash away the emotions she'd brought to the surface. He had to stop this. He couldn't let a simple thank-you make him go all weak in the knees.

He pulled the car under the hospital awning, and before he could open the door, Kat was climbing in. She slid in slowly and with great care, a pained expression on her face that helped douse any positive feelings he had.

All of this was his fault. He'd let a killer get close to her, and he had to live with the thought that she was hurting because he'd failed her.

"You get any pain meds?" he asked as he put the car in gear and headed for the exit.

"I have a prescription, but pain meds always make me sleepy so I'm not going to take any."

"We should get it filled for tonight, though, or you may not sleep well."

"I guess. If we have time."

They had time. Plenty of time to make sure she got a good night's sleep. They were at a hospital so there had to be a pharmacy nearby. He merged onto the main road, making sure they weren't followed and searched the strip malls for a drug store.

"Where are we going?" she asked.

"First the pain meds."

"That can wait."

"It can, but I won't let it." His words came out more forceful than he wanted, but he'd let her get hurt and was going to do the only thing he knew to make it better. At least physically better for her.

She eyed him up for a long moment then seemed resolved to do as he wanted. "Then where?"

"I thought you might like to stop by your place to pick up some clothes for tomorrow." His tone was free from the guilt and deception eating at his gut, but he couldn't look at her. If he told her that her family was waiting for them, he knew she'd figure out a way to avoid going to her house. Besides, he wasn't exactly lying about the reason for going there. He was just omitting the fact that her whole family would be waiting for them.

Right, Elliot. Keep telling yourself that and maybe you'll believe it.

"What I'd like to do," she said, shifting on the seat and looking out her window, "is to go back to Nancy's house and search the files."

"Tommy's got that covered." He made sure she knew this wasn't optional.

Her stomach grumbled. She laughed and glanced at him. "Guess what I really need is something to eat. I can rustle something up at my house."

He gave her a sincere smile. Sincere, anyway, in that he was glad they'd moved past his half-truths. "Any particular pharmacy you use?"

"I rarely get prescriptions filled so it doesn't matter." Her focus was on the window again.

He spotted a chain drugstore down the street. "How about the one on the corner?"

She looked ahead. "Yeah, sure. It'll work."

He flipped on his blinkers and maneuvered into the turn lane. She was still looking out her window as he pulled into the parking lot.

"Something interesting out there?"

"Just making sure no one followed us from the hospital."

"Once a cop, always a cop," he said, and she nodded.

"You can wait out here if you want." She opened the door and climbed out.

"Wait," he said as the door slammed.

She hadn't learned anything from the shooting and apparently, she didn't remember the agreement they'd made on Nancy's porch.

He jumped out and caught up to her. "I guess you've already forgotten that promise to stay by my side."

"Relax. I will when it's necessary. But I made sure we weren't followed and it's a random stop. No one could know we were coming here." For a long moment, she looked up at him, then turned and entered the store.

He hated to admit it, but she had a point. Still, the shooting had scared him too much to let his guard down at all. He could have lost her before he really got to know her, and at this moment, never really knowing her seemed like the worst thing that could happen in his life.

Prescription in hand, Kat shifted into a comfortable position in the front seat of Mitch's car and glanced at him. He hadn't spoken to her since they'd entered the pharmacy. He'd called Tommy to check the progress in locating Nathan's threat file. They'd also talked about investigating Nancy's client list and the source of the propofol. She guessed from hearing Mitch's side of the conversation that Tommy had nothing new to report. Not that Mitch felt a need to fill her in. After he'd hung up, he'd sat stoically next to her until she claimed the prescription and then he'd quietly held the door for her when they'd left.

As they'd traveled toward her town house, she'd tried to keep the mood light and make sure he knew she'd be fine just as Tommy suggested, but something was eating at Mitch. The uncomfortable silence was starting to bother her and she couldn't keep quiet.

"Is everything okay?" she asked lightly.

"You mean other than the fact that I let someone shoot you on my watch?" His voice was low and tormented, and he didn't look at her. "Yeah, it's peachy."

"It wasn't your fault." She stared at him until he looked at her. His face was tense and drawn, and she felt an overwhelming desire to make him feel better. She touched his arm. He winced and she pulled back. "You're hurt. You should have had it looked at."

"It's nothing."

"Somehow, I don't think 'nothing' would make you wince."

"I'm good, Kat."

"You'd tell me if you weren't?"

He laughed and the tension in the space seemed to lighten. "Probably not."

She held her hand over his forearm. "Is it safe to touch you here?"

He nodded, letting his eyes meet hers. She saw the heart-rending tenderness in his gaze. She was overcome with gratitude for all he'd done and all that he would do until this case was resolved. "I am forever in your debt for risking your life and for being here for me. I don't know how I would have gotten through any of this without you."

The warmth fled from his eyes, and the tensing of his jaw further cemented his changed demeanor.

"What did I say?" she asked.

His face clouded with apprehension. "I hope you know that I wouldn't do anything I didn't think was in your best interest."

He'd said the same thing yesterday then refused to let her go home last night. She felt unease welling up inside. "What have you done?"

He pointed out the front window. She saw cars parked outside her town house. Family cars. Justice Agency vehicles.

"You called them." She flashed her gaze up to him. "How could you?"

"We can't do this alone anymore, Kat. The department doesn't have the resources needed to work this case and protect you, too. We need help."

"No."

"I'm afraid there's no choice." He pulled to the curb.

She wanted to bolt, but not before she set him straight on this. "Of course there's a choice." She saw Cole storm out of the house so she rushed on before he interrupted them. "Or at least there *was* a choice before you called them behind my back and took it away from me."

"I'm sorry, Kat," he said, his voice sincere and racked with guilt.

But what difference did that make? Her father had been

sorry, too. Each time he beat her mother, he'd begged for forgiveness. And she'd given it. Then he'd gone right back to taking away all of her choices in life. Telling her what to do. Stifling her. Controlling her. And now Mitch wanted to do the same thing.

Cole ripped open her door and glared down on her. "What were you thinking not telling us about any of this?"

She eased out of the car, but didn't have the strength to answer.

"Are you okay?" He searched her from head to toe, and she nodded, feeling guilty for not telling him what was going on. Maybe she'd been doing a little bit of controlling others, too. But that was different. It was motivated by love.

He swept her into a gentle hug. "Man, Kat, you scared us all to death."

She felt him shudder, and guilt—this time over making them worry about her—brought tears to her eyes. She loved her family and didn't ever want to hurt them. "I'm sorry, Cole. I just didn't want this killer anywhere near all of you."

He leaned back and scolded her with his gaze. "What are we gonna do about you, Kat?" he said fondly. "Our little worrier and protector."

"We could start by getting her inside," Mitch offered, and Cole scowled at him.

"He's right, Cole," she said, surprised she was taking Mitch's side in anything.

They headed up the walk and into the town house. She spotted Dani first who gave her an apologetic smile. Then she saw Dani's twin, Derrick, who resembled his sister except he wore a scowl much like Cole's. She was thankful Ethan was off on his honeymoon with Jennie or there'd be three strong men giving her surly looks. Make that four as Mitch joined them.

"Leave her alone, guys." Dani crossed the room and put a

protective arm around Kat. "She's had enough to deal with without looking at all your grumpy mugs." She smiled at Kat. "Let's go up and pack your things while these guys hash out logistics."

Kat let Dani lead her to the stairs. She felt all three sets of eyes on her so she stiffened her back and climbed the steps. In her room, she crumpled on the bed in exhaustion.

"You don't look so hot." Dani joined her.

"I'll be okay." Kat squeezed her sister's hand. "What about you? They didn't give you any grief did they?"

"All they know is what I told them the other day. They don't know that I spent the night with you last night."

"I won't tell them."

"Better coming from us now. You know it'll come out anyway."

Kat hugged her little sister. "I just don't want them to be mad at you."

"Please. I've survived as the youngest female in the family for years now. I can hold my own." She got up and went to the closet. "So what do you want to pack?"

"It doesn't much matter."

She spun. "Are you kidding me? You want to look your best around Mitch, don't you?"

She groaned as Dani went back to the topic she'd badgered Kat with last night at Mitch's house. "For the last time, Dani, I'm not looking for a relationship."

"Ah, but it's looking for you."

"If you're intimating that Mitch is interested in me, I don't care. He is the bossiest man I know. He makes Ethan look like a softy."

"Mmm-hmm," Dani said, sliding hangers along the pole.

"You're not even listening to me."

"Yes, I am." Dani pulled out a vibrant red dress that Kat had worn to a formal awards banquet. "This will do nicely."

Kat snorted and got up. "Like I'd wear that slinky dress to investigate a murder."

"Well, at least I got you over here to choose your own things, now, didn't I?"

Kat gave her sister a playful sock in the arm, and Dani slipped it around Kat's shoulder. "Don't ever get shot again, Kat. I can survive in an all-male family, but I sure don't want to." Her tone was filled with humor but tears welled in her eyes.

"Not to worry, Squirt," Kat said with a smile in her voice. "I don't plan on letting this killer get that close to me again."

She put the red dress back into the closet and selected more practical clothes that Dani then packed into an overnight bag.

"I need to grab a few things from the bathroom." She went down the hallway to the only bathroom in the two-bedroom town house.

The scent of a man's cologne stopped her dead in her tracks. This was the same fragrance the killer wore. The same cloying, sickly scent that had overpowered her as he'd tried to stab a needle into her arm.

She drew her weapon and backed out, moving quietly down the hall to the spare bedroom. She put one foot in front of the other as her heart tripped at a fast rate.

His nauseating scent didn't linger in the air in here, but she wasn't taking any chances. She cautiously approached the closet door and whipped it open.

Empty.

She searched behind the door and under the bed.

No one.

With her family downstairs, he couldn't be down there. He was gone.

The curtain fluttered and she went to the window for the first time realizing it was cold in here. The window was open behind the blinds, the screen knocked out. She leaned out.

He must have been in the house when her family arrived and shimmied down the thick drainpipe, then dropped onto the roof of the back porch to escape.

Careful to disturb as little evidence as possible, she went back down the hall to get her bag. She didn't want to tell anyone that he'd been here, but she had no choice. If she wanted to stay alive, she had to share with the family that the killer had gotten closer and even more personal. And for the first time, she was starting to fear he just might succeed in his quest to end her life.

EIGHT

Mitch looked at Kat's brothers. They were angry. Both of them. Cole had his arms crossed and legs planted wide. A hard scowl lurked beneath end-of-the-day stubble, and he ran a hand through hair that could use a trim. The younger brother was less intimidating. He was taller and leaner, but with the way his T-shirt fit, Mitch knew there would be power in his fist if he decided to aim one his way.

His best bet was to get them to focus on protecting Kat and maybe that would diffuse their anger at him for failing to involve them before their sister was shot. "I could use your help investigating Nathan Bodig's clients. Nancy's list, too. It would speed up the investigation."

"We can do that," Derrick offered. "In fact, we'll take over everything related to Kat and you can be on your way." He resumed glaring.

"Look," Mitch said, feeling as if he was talking to a brick wall. "We all have the same goal here. To catch this killer so he can't hurt Kat again. Glaring at me like this or trying to cut me out isn't going to make that any easier."

"She could've died," Cole said matter-of-factly.

"Don't you think I know that?" Mitch's voice rose, and he felt the fear from the afternoon return. "I'd never want Kat to get hurt. Never."

Cole raised a brow and appraised Mitch with ice-blue eyes. "You care about her, don't you?"

"Yes," Mitch admitted and hoped they wouldn't ask what his intentions were, as he hadn't a clue, and he didn't want to make the two of them madder.

Cole looked at Derrick and the younger brother gave a clipped nod. "Then I guess we can work together on this."

"Just to clarify," Mitch said and met their gazes one at a time. "I'm officially in charge of this case, and I'm simply asking for your help. I'll have the final say on any plans involving Kat's safety."

"We'll play it by ear," Cole said.

"This isn't negotiable," Mitch warned.

"Fine," Cole said, but his focus had drifted to Kat and Dani coming down the stairs.

Mitch wondered if this agreement was because he didn't want to argue in front of Kat or if Cole really would keep his word. Mitch would need to be alert to make sure Cole didn't try to outmaneuver him.

He turned his attention to the sisters and instantly knew from Kat's tight expression that something had happened upstairs. He met her at the bottom of the stairs. "What is it? What happened?"

"He was here."

"Who? The killer?"

She nodded, but looked at her brothers. "I smelled his cologne in the bathroom. I cleared the upstairs and found the window in the spare bedroom open. He must have been here when you all arrived then bailed out the window." She sounded calm and collected, but he saw her hand tremble.

That now-familiar urge to comfort her rose up, but after what she'd said about trying to prove herself while working with her brothers, he didn't want to make her seem weak. Plus after calling in her family without her approval, he'd be lucky if she had a conversation with him again much less let him touch her.

Cole drew his weapon and headed toward the back of the house. "I doubt he's still here, but we can't be too careful."

"I'll get F.E.D. out here." Mitch dialed the Forensics Evidence Division to arrange for a team to process her town house. Maybe they'd get luckier than they had with the fingerprints from Nancy's house where Tommy still hadn't hit on any prints.

As he requested assistance, he heard Derrick questioning Kat. Her answers came out clipped and rapid like the bullets fired at her earlier. She was more upset than she let anyone know. He wondered if her siblings could tell how unsettled she was or if he was the only one who could read her so well. And he *could* read her.

How had he gotten this close to her in just a few days?

He hung up and felt his heart tighten at the pain dulling those amazing eyes. She'd been through so much, and he wanted to whisk her away somewhere safe. Lock her in a safe house and throw away the key.

"We're clear," Cole announced as he came back into the room and holstered his weapon.

"Perhaps it's time to locate a safe house for Kat." Mitch didn't have the heart to look at her as he said it. He knew his suggestion would cause her additional pain and he didn't want to see it.

"No!" she said. "I'm not going anywhere."

"That might be a good idea, Kat," Cole said, and Mitch glanced at her then.

"I said no." She looked so disappointed in him. "I'm not one of our helpless clients. I know how to protect myself."

"Like you did this afternoon?" The minute the words came out of his mouth Mitch wished he could take them back. She glared at him with such venom it felt like a slap across the face.

Dani stepped between them. "Kat has made her wishes known. There are four of us to work her protection detail now. Five, counting Tommy. Why don't we focus on how we can help her out and still let her participate in this investigation?"

"First off, we should move this discussion to the office," Derrick suggested. "It'll get Kat somewhere safe for now and F.E.D. will be able to do their job."

"Works for me," Cole said, and looked at Mitch. "That okay with you?"

Mitch nodded and Cole faced Derrick. "How about retrieving the vests from the car?"

After a glance at Kat, Derrick gave a sober nod and left the house. Mitch couldn't stand here and see Kat's fisted hands or her stoic posture. He had to talk to her. To explain his reasoning for suggesting a safe house. He took her elbow to move her away so they could talk privately. She shook off his hand, but followed him.

"You're angry with me," he said softly so the others wouldn't hear.

"You bet I am." She didn't keep her voice down at all and they turned to look at him. "It was bad enough that you called my family without asking me first, but then your comment about this afternoon? It was uncalled for and just plain mean."

She was right. He'd been mean when he'd only wanted to help. "That's not how I meant it, Kat. It's just this afternoon when I saw you there on the porch, I—" His voice broke so he stopped to get control of his emotions before going on. "I can't let you get hurt again, Kat. I just can't."

"I don't care why you did it, you did it and I'm not sure I can ever trust you again." Her voice was cold with anger.

She walked away from him, and his gut twisted. He'd known she'd react badly, but the reality was far worse than he expected.

Derrick came back inside carrying a pile of bulletproof

vests and tossed them to everyone except Kat. He carried hers across the room. "I'll help you so you don't have to lift your injured arm."

"I can help her," Mitch offered, but she wouldn't even look at him.

As Derrick slipped the vest over her head, Mitch stood there, waiting for a word, any word that she might forgive him. She didn't say a thing.

When her vest was settled, Mitch kept his tone light and smiled. "Ready to go?"

"I'm riding with Cole."

"Don't do this, Kat."

"Do what?" she whispered. "Go with someone else so you can't boss me around every second of every day?"

"I thought that was one of things that bothered you most about working with your family."

"They may not give me many dangerous assignments, but they don't try to control my every move." She walked away, her back rigid and strong.

Cole had caught the interaction and stood watching them with his eyebrow lifted, but other than that, Mitch couldn't read her brother's face. He clearly hid his emotions well, like Mitch did. At least like Mitch did when Kat wasn't around. She brought them all to the surface.

Maybe it was a good idea for her to go with someone like Cole who could hold his feelings in check. For Mitch to stay here so no one was distracted by their personal issues. He listened as they planned the exit from the town house. The security detail sounded well thought out and obviously something they'd done many times before. Kat was safe with them.

"You coming, Elliot?" Cole met Mitch's gaze.

"I'll hang out here until F.E.D. arrives," Mitch said, trying to sound convincing but hoping Kat would argue. She didn't even turn to look at him so he said, "I'll stop by the agency later."

"You okay with bringing her suitcase when you come?" Cole asked. "Frees up our hands."

Mitch nodded and watched them exit. The Justice family, strong, together and focused. All the things he'd failed to be for Kat. Despair swallowed him, just as it had earlier today when he saw Kat lying on the porch. His gut ached with emptiness, reminding him of the way he'd felt before getting to know her. The way he'd lived for so long and the way that thanks to a cute, spunky little woman, he'd never be able to go back to when this was all over. Trouble was, the fear of going forward still outweighed the sadness of the past.

As they moved toward Cole's SUV, Kat knew how the filling in a sandwich felt. Derrick led the team, Cole moved close to her side and Dani brought up the rear. She'd worked this kind of transport detail before, just never as the protectee and it seemed odd.

As they walked, routine took over and she kept her head on a swivel watching for the glint of a weapon or any movement in the trees. Despite her unease, nothing untoward happened and they settled in Cole's car just as it started raining.

"You okay, Kit Kat?" Cole glanced at her as he turned the ignition.

"I'm fine," she answered, even though the way he'd said her nickname so affectionately brought tears to her eyes.

In less than a minute, their convoy—led by Derrick with Dani at the rear—was on the road. She looked out the window and watched the soft drizzle darken the pavement as mile after mile flew by. The gloomy afternoon was much like her mood. A few days and her life had fallen apart.

How had everything gotten so screwed up so fast? How had she started to fall for a man so like her birth father? Mitch was so pushy and domineering that she never wanted to see him again and yet she had to concentrate hard to keep her eyes off him at the house.

She sighed.

"That bad, huh?" Cole gave her a quick glance.

"Maybe worse."

"Want to tell me about it?"

She swiveled toward him. "Why do some guys have to control every little thing?"

"Some guys?" He laughed. "Don't you mean most guys?"

"Some are worse than others."

"I take it you're talking about Elliot."

"Yeah."

"Sometimes it's hard being a guy, Kat. We have to be tough to make it in the world. So being in charge becomes second nature. Especially for men in law enforcement. You know we're taught to protect life at all costs. And that doesn't usually give us a lot of time to think about the warm fuzzies of a situation. We just act."

"Are you lumping yourself in the same category as Mitch?"

"Depends on what category you're putting him in." He cast an appraising look her way. "If you think he's like your birth father, berating a woman and demeaning her until she does what he wants, then no, I'm not like that. But if you're talking about doing everything within my power to protect someone I care about, then yes, I'm very much like that and you know it."

And that was what Mitch was like, too. Plus kind and warm, generous, and…she could go on and on, but she was beginning to sound like a woman falling in love and that didn't sit well with her.

"You know—" Cole gave her a long hard look "—you're no different than Mitch. You want to control everyone around you, too."

"Funny, Cole."

"I'm not kidding. Whenever there's the least bit of chance we could get hurt, you try to take charge. Even if it means not telling us a killer's threatening your life."

"That's different."

"Oh, really? Remember when you tried to warn off Jennie last year when she came back into Ethan's life? If she would've listened to you, she and Ethan would never have gotten together again."

"Well...I..."

"What's the matter, Kat? Don't like it when you see it in yourself?"

"No... I mean...it's just... It's different. I do it out of love for you guys. Not just to push you around."

He clicked on his blinker and turned onto the tree-lined street that was home to their office. "Are you so sure Elliot's just trying to push you around? Maybe he cares about you."

"He hardly knows me."

"Ahh, but that's not stopping you from falling for him is it?"

"It's not like that."

"Then how is it?"

She sighed. "I don't know, Cole. I just don't know anything anymore."

He laughed and parked in front of their office. "That, my little sister, is the first sign that you're not really bothered by his behavior but more bothered by how you're reacting to him." He met her gaze again. "This is what you've always done in your relationships. You're trying to push him out of your life. After seeing your father dominate your mother, you're just too afraid to let a man have any power over you."

He jumped out, and Kat thought about Cole while waiting for her siblings to join them. Since coming back from Iraq, Cole could be counted on to cut to the quick of everyone's issues but his own. He was so sullen and unhappy now, rarely cracking a smile or joking with them as he once had. He'd only been back from Iraq for a few weeks before their parents had been murdered. He could use some time by himself to sort things out and once this whole mess was over she'd talk to her siblings and stage an intervention to make sure he got that time.

She was brought up short as she realized she was behaving just the way Cole had said—taking charge when it came to the people she wanted to protect. She pushed the thought away.

He opened her door and they all hurried through the dropping temperature, the rain hitting her face as cold as ice pellets.

"We'll meet in the conference room," Cole announced from the landing as the others tromped up the stairs.

"You guys go ahead," Dani said. "I'm going to place a pizza order."

"No black olives," Derrick reminded his twin as if she didn't already know all of his likes and dislikes.

"I'll make sure she gets the order right," Kat said, hoping to talk with her sister. She grabbed Dani's arm and steered her into the main office.

Dani turned and raised a finely plucked brow. "What's going on?"

"Am I a control freak?" Kat asked.

Her perfectly girly, perfectly ladylike sister snorted, then laughed, and Kat impaled her with a sharp stare.

"Oh, wait," Dani said, still smiling. "You're serious."

"Of course I am."

"It's just, I thought you knew that by now."

Kat put her hands on hips. "I realize I like things my way, but I'm not one of those people who takes over all the time, am I?"

Dani's brows rose again. "Why are you questioning this all of a sudden?"

"I was talking to Cole about how Mitch is so bossy and decides everything for me. And Cole said I was just like Mitch."

Dani laid a hand on Kat's shoulder. "I'm sorry if you don't like hearing that, sweetie, but it's true. At least when it comes to all of us."

"But that's not a bad thing, is it?"

"Depends, I guess. If you're jumping in because you don't trust God to work things out in His time and His way, then, yeah, it's not only bad, it's a sin."

"But He doesn't want us to just sit around and do nothing. He gave us the ability to take care of ourselves."

"Of course, but He also doesn't want us to step ahead of Him or worry about things that are out of our hands." Dani paused and put her arm around Kat. "And you, my sweet sister, worry all the time."

She did. They were right. She tried to control things, and she did worry. Constantly. She didn't trust God's plans. Probably never had really trusted Him. And that was wrong. Sinful, like Dani said. She had to change.

"Kat?"

Maybe admitting the problem was the first step. "I really thought I was open to God's plans for my life, but in all honesty, I try to take charge of things to protect myself from pain." She shook her head. "I can't believe I didn't see how wrong it is."

"Hey, don't be so hard on yourself. It's difficult to trust that God knows what's best when sometimes His best involves pain. We just have to take things one at a time." She squeezed again, then let go. "And right now, our next thing is feeding the hungry horde known as our brothers. So let's get that pizza ordered." She logged on to the computer, and Kat perched on the desk and raised her face in prayer.

Father, forgive me for worrying and not trusting You. Help me fully to trust You to do what is best for me. And Lord, if that means letting go and letting a man into my life, let me be open to that, too.

She looked back at Dani. A lighthearted, trusting, accepting person. Someone Kat could use as a role model for learning how to leave her problems with God and let Him take charge. Even important life-altering things like asking God to help her be open to a relationship.

Could she really trust that Mitch was the wonderful man he seemed to be?

"This look okay to you?" Dani asked, pointing at the screen.

Kat reviewed the order. "Looks good."

Dani clicked Send and turned. "Looks like you're still thinking about our discussion."

"I am." Kat pushed off the desk and Dani slung an arm around her shoulders again.

"You're not beating yourself up about it, are you?"

"No. Just hoping I can find a way to get over this."

Dani smiled. "I know you can do it."

Not as certain she could do this, Kat still smiled up at Dani and hoped that her sister's confidence was well placed.

NINE

Mitch arrived at the Justice Agency and found the door locked. He rang a buzzer and waited, shoving his hands into his pockets to keep them warm. He could be in for an interesting drive home tonight if the rain kept up and the temperature continued downward.

He counted to thirty and when no one came to the lobby, he pounded on the glass. As soon as Kat had walked out of her town house with her family, he'd known he'd made a mistake in not accompanying her. As the officer in charge of this case, he was tasked with her protection and he never should've let his feelings get the best of him or let her leave without him.

Still no answer. He dug out his cell and dialed Kat.

"Mitch," she answered, her voice as frosty as before.

"I'm at the door. Can someone let me in?" It came out terse, and he didn't blame her when she hung up on him without a word. He'd meant to apologize to her. To explain why he was behaving like a pigheaded guy. But the chilly tone in her voice set him off again.

After a few more minutes, Cole came down the hallway and unlocked the door. "F.E.D. find anything?" he asked before Mitch could step inside.

"They lifted shoe prints near the patio. Men's athletic shoe, size ten."

"A common size. Won't likely be a lot of help, then." He turned the lock with a solid click.

"Exactly." Mitch climbed the stairs. "You have any luck with the client lists?'

"Since Nancy worked strictly with businesses and we wanted to catch Nathan's clients at home tonight, we started with Nathan's list. We've pared it down to clients who've committed violent crimes and we've managed to locate a good number of them. We'll head out and talk to them after we finish our pizza."

"You're not planning to let Kat tag along, are you?"

Cole stopped walking and met his gaze. "I was hoping you'd keep her company here."

Mitch stifled his surprise. "I'm glad to oblige, but are you sure Kat will agree to that?"

Cole laughed. "No, she'll fight it all the way, but I think it'd be good if the two of you had some private time to work out whatever's causing stress between you. Stress leads to accidents and accidents lead to death."

Mitch eyed up Cole. "You saying it was my fault she was hit this morning?"

"Not at all. I just don't want it to be a problem in the future." Cole studied Mitch. "Look, Elliot, Kat has some issues with control. As in, she has to be in charge. Whenever she gets pushed, she fights back. Remember that when you talk to her." Cole continued down the hallway.

Mitch expected Cole to be harder on him, but the guy seemed all right. Some of Mitch's unease over stepping into the middle of her family again abated.

Cole turned into a room at the end of the hallway, and Mitch followed, his stomach rumbling at the smell of food. He found the family seated at a long conference table, two nearly devoured pizzas in the middle. Conversation stopped and they looked at him as if he were an alien. Kat gave him an irritated look, and he *felt* as if he were an alien.

"Help yourself to pizza," Dani offered.

He didn't hesitate but took a paper plate. The only open chair other than the one at Kat's side was across from her. He didn't want to see her scowl at him while he ate so he sat next to her.

"You want soda, water or coffee?" Dani asked.

"Water's great. Thanks."

She went to a small fridge on the counter lining the far wall and pulled out a bottle. Obviously, she was the hostess of the family.

"Glad you could join us." She handed it to him and returned to her seat.

Cracking open the bottle, Mitch looked around the table. Other than the twins, the siblings were so different-looking—not surprising since they were all adopted—and yet there was a family unity that made Mitch jealous.

"So Ethan called this morning," Dani said.

Derrick rolled his eyes. "Seriously? On his honeymoon? That guy has got to get his priorities straight."

"Jennie will set him straight soon enough." Cole's voice held no humor.

"C'mon, Cole," Dani said, shaking her head. "You make it sound like he's serving a prison sentence instead of being married to the woman he loves."

"Sometimes being with the one you love *is* a prison sentence." Kat sounded even more dour than Cole. Thinking she might mean him, Mitch waited for her to turn and glare at him, but she didn't move.

"I can't believe either of you can talk like that with the way Mom and Dad raised us." Dani was still shaking her head.

"If you get burned by love you'll change your tune." Cole slid his plate away and drained his soda before standing.

"Time to hit the road. Kat, you'll stay here with Mitch and the rest of us will knock on some doors."

Her eyes flashed wide in surprise. "You can't be serious."

"That I am."

"I think we should put this to a vote."

"Fine." He looked at his siblings. "All in favor of Kat and Mitch holding down the fort raise your hand?"

All hands went up.

"You set me up."

Cole smiled, something Mitch didn't think the guy was capable of. "That I did."

Dani got up and patted Kat on the back. "It's for your own good."

"Et tu, Brute?"

"Me, too, sis. Me, too." She bent down and whispered something Mitch didn't catch, but it made Kat's face color, and she swatted at her sister.

As the family exited the room, Mitch felt Kat's eyes on him so he swallowed his bite of pizza that suddenly tasted like cardboard. "You're still mad at me."

"You think?"

He did look at her then, and at the sight of her disapproving glare, he wished he hadn't. "I was just trying to do the right thing, Kat. We needed your family's help."

"We could've done this on our own."

"The killer nearly took you out today. We needed additional manpower and resources."

She paused and assessed him for long moments, then sighed. "Maybe you're right. Maybe we did, but you know how I feel about putting my family in danger." She crossed her arms. "Making sure our family members are safe is the *one* thing I thought you and I agreed on."

"It is. I'll do everything I can to safeguard the people I care about." He took a deep breath and waited until she was looking into his eyes. "But I care about you, too. That's why I had to call them." He didn't know how he expected her to react to his admission, but sitting perfectly still and staring at him, her eyes unreadable wasn't the response he'd have predicted.

He opened his mouth to ask what she was thinking, but his cell vibrated on the table, and he glanced at it.

"It's Tommy." Wishing they could've worked this out before duty called again, he punched his speaker button. "Go ahead, Tommy. You're on speaker."

"Good news. I located Bodig's threat file."

"That is good news," Kat said.

"So there are three items in the folder," Tommy continued. "One of them seems really credible."

Kat jumped up and grabbed a stack of papers from the end of the table. "I have the client list. What name am I looking for?"

"I don't have a last name, but the father's first name is Ray. The son is deceased so he may not be on the list, but his name is Paul."

"Depending on when that threat was written, they could still be here," Kat said, already running her finger down a page.

"It's a little more than sixty days old," Tommy replied.

Kat flipped the page. "This list has Nathan's clients for the past ninety days so odds are good we'll find a Paul on it."

"I'd really like to get a look at that letter, Tommy," Mitch said, excitement starting to build. "Any chance you'd bring it over to the Justice Agency?"

"I can do that. I'll be there in less than ten."

"Text me when you arrive and I'll let you in." Mitch clicked off his phone and the excitement flamed up a few notches before he tamped it down. He knew better than to be encouraged by such a small lead and normally he wouldn't get this worked up, but sitting next to a woman who was coming to mean a lot to him and was flaming angry with him, he'd take every little bit of encouragement he could find.

Kat turned the page and felt Mitch's eyes on her, but she kept reading. The sooner she found Paul and Ray, the sooner this could end and she could go back to her old life, free of Mitch Elliot and the effect he continued to have on her emotions.

"Are you trying to burn a hole in me?" she asked without looking up and losing her place on the page.

"I'm sorry, you know," he said, his voice holding an honest apology. "I should never have called Cole without telling you about it first."

She marked her spot with a pen, then looked up to search the depth of his eyes for any hint of duplicity. He laid a hand on hers, and she felt her heart thawing despite her desire to stay mad. "I can't let anything happen to you, Kat."

She sat there mesmerized by the extent of caring in his eyes and the touch of his hand. Not sure what to say or how to act.

"Here's the thing." He abruptly pulled away and sat back. "When I saw you lying on the porch not moving, I flashed back to Lori. And I admit it. I panicked. Without thinking things through, I called Cole."

So this was about Lori. Suddenly Kat needed to know the whole story. "What happened to Lori? I mean you mentioned her before but didn't give any details."

He closed his eyes and looked up.

"You don't have to tell me if you don't want to," she said, hoping he'd ignore the out she was giving him.

"No...no... It's okay." He took a deep breath. "It was a simple domestic call. I'd surprised Lori the night before with an engagement ring. On the way to the call we were trying to come up with a date for our wedding."

"So you were involved with her." Kat didn't know why the thought of that hurt, but it did.

He held up his hands. "Before you say anything about dating your partner, I know it can cloud judgment in dangerous situations. We were holding off telling our supervisor about our relationship until we knew it would work out. We'd planned to tell him about the engagement at the end of our shift."

Not where she was going with this, but he was right. The rules against dating your partner existed for a reason. "Go on."

"We arrived at the house. It was quiet. No sign of a disturbance. Lori was so pumped over our engagement, she almost floated to the door. I trailed a few seconds behind her." He shook his head and closed his eyes for a second as if it would make the sight of what came next go away. "She made it as far as the steps. The male in the dispute was drunk, and he came barreling out of the house with a shotgun. Without warning he blasted her in the chest." He took another deep breath. "Before I could even draw my weapon he got off another shot, and I went down."

"You were hit, too?" Kat felt her heart nearly stop beating. "Where?"

He tipped his head to the side and dragged a finger over a scar running from chin to collarbone right next to his carotid artery. She couldn't believe she was having this conversation with him. Or the way it made her feel sick to her stomach.

Without thinking, she traced her finger over the scar. "You were lucky, Mitch. A little to the right and you would've bled out in less than a minute."

"Not sure how lucky I was to watch Lori take her last breath."

Kat rested her hand on his arm. "I'm so sorry, Mitch."

"It was hard, you know. I mean, I still keep asking why I

lived, and she didn't." He looked up and shook his head. "I still second-guess everything about that day. Did our relationship have anything to do with her death? Could I have done anything differently? If I had, would she still be alive?"

"Did I.A. clear you?" Kat asked, knowing Internal Affairs investigated all shootings.

"Yeah."

"No one has more exacting standards in an investigation than I.A., Mitch. If they cleared you then you didn't do anything wrong and you can't think this way." She thought about the guilt she still carried over her mother's death. Letting that remorse control you was no way to live. "You have to let it go, before it eats you up inside."

He appraised her, his gaze a silent question. "Sounds as if you're speaking from experience."

"I am," she said, though she'd rather not bring up her past.

He looked at her as if he were weighing her response. "There weren't any officers slain while you were on the force."

"No, not on the job."

"Oh, right," he nodded, understanding dawning on his face. "The Justices. Losing your parents that way was a terrible thing, Kat. I hope you know how sorry I am about that."

"Thank you," she said and considered letting him think this was what was bothering her. But he'd been so open, so honest with her it was only fair that she explain. "But actually I was thinking about my birth mother." Kat hadn't talked about her mom in years, so when tears pricked her eyes, it caught her by surprise. "My father killed her."

He didn't say anything for a moment, but took her hand in his. "That must have been hard. How old were you?"

She couldn't keep looking at his tender gaze without crying so she focused on the pipes running across the ceiling. "I was eleven when she died, but he'd abused her for years before that. I tried to get her to leave him. She wouldn't. She kept thinking he'd change."

"But he didn't," he said with so much empathy that she had the courage to look at him again.

"No, he didn't," she repeated. "He really lost it that night. I didn't even know he had a gun, but he pulled one out of his dresser and aimed at my mom. I jumped him from behind, but he shrugged me off and fired. When she fell, I ran over there, but he just stood there his mouth gaping open." As the memories assaulted her, she shook her head. "It was so odd. Surreal really. He started to cry, and he looked so lost. I almost wanted to give him a hug. Seriously, how could I want to hug a man who'd just killed my mom?"

"He was your father." Mitch sandwiched her hand between both of his, the warmth thawing some of the chill surrounding her heart.

"Not much of one." She looked at their hands and tried to find something positive to say.

"But still, he was your father."

"He was. Until he turned the gun on himself. Then he was just a sad, pitiful man who'd ruined my life." Tears starting to fall, she looked up at Mitch. Her heart clenched at the tender concern in his eyes. "I lost my whole family in one night."

He slid his chair closer and turned her by the shoulders so she was facing him. "This is why you're always so afraid of your family getting hurt."

"Partly," she said, wanting to stop talking about this but also wanting to get it out and move on with life. "But honestly, I always knew my dad would go too far someday and something bad would happen." She shook her head again. "That sounds horrible, doesn't it? I knew he was going to kill her and yet I didn't find a way to stop it."

He scooted even closer, and he wiped away a tear with a

gentle finger then settled his hands on her knees. "You were only eleven, Kat. Just a child."

"And yet—"

"And yet you thought you should've been able to save her and now you're afraid you'll fail the people you love."

She nodded. "At least we're all out of law enforcement now and not risking our lives every day."

"Believe me, I get that." His voice rang with sincerity and she knew they were kindred spirits in this. "You want everyone you care about out of harm's way."

"Now if only I could get Tommy to retire." *And you, too,* she thought, wondering what it would be like to be married to a cop and see him head into the line of fire every day. The thought sent a chill down her back. "I don't understand how anyone could marry someone in law enforcement. That's the last thing I'd do. I could never sit around and wait for that death notification call."

His eyes went dark and sad, and he pushed back, straightening his shoulders and holding his body rigid. Her comment clearly bothered him. Was it because he was starting to care for her, or because he was thinking about his prior engagement to a police officer? Did it matter? Not really. Despite her attraction to him, she couldn't commit to a man with such a dangerous job. She was starting to accept that some things were out of her control but giving into her feelings for Mitch wasn't one of them. This was her choice and she chose to keep her heart safe.

TEN

"There's no Paul on the list." Kat dropped the papers, clearly frustrated. Mitch knew that he should feel the same way but he was still distracted by her bomb about never marrying a police officer. He couldn't let it go.

She told him this, just when he was ready to admit for the first time since losing Lori, he wanted more in life than being on his own. Maybe with Kat. But now he knew he had no chance with her. None. Not if he was a detective, and he'd never leave his job. Not as long as there were potential murderers with little regard for life out there like the man who killed Lori.

His phone chimed, and Kat jumped.

"That'll be Tommy." Mitch smiled as he rose, but it was hard to make his lips turn up. "I'll let him in."

The conversation kept running through his head as he headed down the hallway. Kat may have ended any notion of a relationship between them, but at least he now understood why she hated for anyone to tell her what to do. Why she had control issues, as Cole said. And why she said being married to someone you love could be a prison sentence. She wasn't talking about the thought of being with him, she was speaking of her father.

And Mitch had repeatedly behaved just like her father and

told her what to do. Maybe he could cut back on giving directions. Maybe ask instead of tell. At least he planned to try.

He jogged down the stairs to the door. He smiled in earnest when he saw Tommy stomping his feet outside trying to stay warm. His partner hated the cold, and keeping him waiting was bound to irritate him.

Mitch turned the lock and felt a blast of cold air mixed with drizzle. "Roads still okay?"

"Yeah, but not for long." Tommy shivered as he stepped inside while holding several plastic evidence bags.

"I hope they hold out. I can't imagine the mess I'll find from Princess if I get stuck here tonight."

"We could head to your place right now."

"I need to stay here with Kat."

Tommy quirked a brow. "Where's the family?"

"They're out knocking on doors of Bodig's clients."

Tommy stopped and caught Mitch's gaze. "And Ethan left you in charge of his sister?"

"He's on his honeymoon."

"Okay, so Cole then."

"Yeah, he's cool."

Tommy's mouth dropped open. "Cole? We're talking about Cole Justice?"

Mitch laughed. "Yeah, why?"

"Since he came back from his second tour, he hasn't said more than two words to me. Kat says he's really struggling to acclimate into civilian life again."

"He seemed okay to me." Mitch started walking again and Tommy caught up to him.

"So was Paul on the client list?" Tommy asked.

"No Paul or Ray."

Tommy caught Mitch's gaze. "You think Bodig's boss played us?"

Mitch shrugged. "He didn't seem to be hiding anything but he wasn't overly cooperative, either."

They went into the conference room and Tommy gave Kat a jab to her good arm, which Mitch was beginning to notice his partner always did when he greeted her. "You look like you could use some sleep."

"Didn't your mother teach you not to tell a woman she looks tired?" She smiled up at him, a smile Mitch also noticed she reserved for those she truly cared about.

"You?" He grinned. "You're not a woman. You're my ex-partner."

"Can I see the threat?" Mitch asked, wishing he'd been on the end of one of those private smiles.

Tommy flipped through the evidence bags and handed one to Mitch, then straddled a chair next to Kat. "Basically Paul was busted for possession. The dad thought the kid should've gotten probation, but Bodig recommended incarceration. He thought the dad was unfit and the kid needed to get out of the home."

"So how'd Paul die?" Kat asked.

"Killed in an altercation in lockup."

"So we have a dad who thinks Nathan's decision could've gotten his son killed," she said, her voice full of enthusiasm.

"A good motive for murder if ever I saw one," Mitch said, catching her enthusiasm. "Now all we have to do is figure out Ray's and Paul's identities."

"We should be able to run Paul down pretty easily," Tommy said. "Can't be that many kids killed in lockup."

"Would be faster for me to put pressure on Weichert in the morning to see if he left this one off the list on purpose," Mitch said.

"You think he's covering something up?" Kat asked, her eyebrow rising.

"I think this threat seems credible, and Weichert said there weren't any credible threats. Makes me think he was trying to hide it." Mitch flipped through the other letters, scanning them for validity then looking at Tommy. "These aren't as compelling, but we need to evaluate them, too. Can you get a warrant for his work email account to see if there are others?"

"With these threats, it shouldn't be a problem," Tommy offered. "I found personal emails in his files, too. I'll request a warrant for both accounts first thing in the morning."

"This should also be all we need to finally get that warrant Weichert's demanding," Mitch added. "I'd rather not talk to Weichert again without the warrant so can you work on that one first?"

"You got it." Tommy gathered the bags together. "Doesn't seem like there's anything else we can do tonight. I suggest we head out before the roads get any worse."

Mitch flashed him a surprised look. After their discussion a few minutes ago, Tommy knew they couldn't leave.

"What?" Tommy stared back. "She'll be safe at your house."

"Looks like the roads are freezing up," Mitch said to Kat, making sure his tone wasn't bossy. "Would you mind coming home with me so I can let Princess out before she makes a mess?"

She eyed him for a few seconds, looking surprised that he was asking instead of telling. Then, even though her expression said she thought better of it, she nodded. "I'll text Cole on the way, and he can pick me up there." She stood and lifted her coat from the back of the chair.

"Vest, please." Mitch nodded at her bulletproof vest.

She didn't argue but put her coat on and slipped the vest over it. Mitch grabbed his jacket, and they all headed down the hall.

At the door, Mitch turned to Kat. "If you don't mind waiting here, I'll pull up the car."

Tommy faked gagging himself. "What happened to you, partner? 'If you don't mind, would you pretty please.' Enough already. I'm gonna be sick."

Kat started laughing, her eyes so alive Mitch had to draw in a breath.

"I never thought I'd say this, but he's right," she said after her laughter stilled. "I like the real Mitch Elliot better." She smiled softly up at him, and when their eyes met, his heart exploded with warmth, and he couldn't look away. The gaze heated up and everything around them blurred. He could look into those honey-brown eyes forever.

Tommy cleared his throat. "Uh…hello? Are you getting the car or are we gonna stand here all night?"

Mitch reluctantly pulled away and with one last look at Kat, he navigated slippery sidewalks to the parking lot. He'd been kind and polite, yet she admitted liking the real him. Maybe there was hope for him after all. He probably shouldn't be thinking this way, but how could he not after that intense gaze.

And her laugh. He smiled as he climbed into his car. A full smile that rang true in her eyes. He could get used to seeing her like that. Actually, he wanted to get used to it—wanted to see her laugh like that again and again.

"Get a grip, Elliot," he mumbled to himself. "It was just a laugh."

He brought his car to the front and noted the sound of the tires crunching over a thin layer of ice. Could be a dicey ride home.

Tommy opened the front door and leaned in, a good-natured smile on his face. "Might want to cool it, partner. Another look like that one and you'll scare her away." He backed out, made a sweeping bow like the gentleman he rarely was and grinned at Kat as she climbed in.

"See you tomorrow, Justice." He shut the door and pounded on the roof.

Mitch navigated the slick streets lined with trees glistening with white ice crystals. But the road was another matter. It was coated with black ice, the dangerous kind of ice. The kind you couldn't always see and prepare for, and mimicking the way he was feeling about Kat. One minute they were sharing longing looks the next he did something stupid, and she wasn't talking to him. Then they were back to the looks, but he didn't really know where they stood.

He glanced at her as she peered out the window. "You never said if I'm forgiven for calling Cole."

She met his gaze, and he made sure his eyes were filled with the sincere contrition he felt.

She shook her head as if she didn't want to forgive him, but she would. "We're good, but don't ever do something like that again."

"I won't," he promised and hoped he could keep his word. A car pulled out ahead of him and as he slowed, the rear end of the SUV fishtailed before he brought it under control.

"The roads are worse than I thought," Kat said, sounding and looking worried.

Not like a former cop to be this concerned about a little ice. At least not for her own safety. He glanced at her and saw the same look as when she'd found out he'd called her family and put them in danger.

Right. The other Justices were on the road.

"You should call them," he encouraged as he eased the car forward. "It's the only thing that'll give you peace."

She focused a narrow-eyed gaze on him. "So now you can read my mind, huh?"

"It's not hard to see you're concerned about your family." He felt her intense study, but concentrated on the icy road. "You'll worry until you know they're fine."

She didn't say anything so he looked at her again. Her eyes had narrowed even more. He'd said something wrong again, but he didn't know what. "Kat?"

"It's okay. I don't need to call them." She spoke with quiet, but desperate firmness.

He slowed at a red light. "I won't think less of you, if that's what's stopping you."

"Actually it's not. I'm trying not to worry so much and trust that God will take care of us."

"Good luck with that." He shot off a quick response, but when a look of uncertainty came over her face, he regretted it.

"You don't think I can do it?" She ended with her cute little jaw angled defiantly.

"I think you can do whatever you set your mind to. I'm the one who can't seem to find solid footing with God again."

She studied him intently. "You know, Mitch Elliot, for a cop, you're a pretty nice guy."

He laughed. "Wish that hadn't been couched with '*for a cop*,' but thanks."

"Wait, I didn't mean it to sound so bad. I meant, cops can sometimes be hard and cold. But you're not."

He winked at her. "You're not so bad yourself."

Color rushed up her neck and over her face, and he couldn't help but smile over the effect he seemed to have on her.

Her phone rang, and she quickly busied her hands by digging it out, but he could see the tough little ex-cop turning a deeper shade of red. Even more charming. Too charming. Strong and soft at the same time.

The light changed, and he shamelessly listened to Kat's conversation with Dani while navigating the slippery streets. Sounded like none of the siblings' visits had produced a lead and they were soon going to call it a night.

She hung up, and he felt her eyes on him again. "It seems

to me," she said, "you know a whole lot about me and I know next to nothing about you."

"Hey!" he protested and gave her a quick smile. "You know that I'm a nice guy."

"Quit avoiding the subject. Tell me more about your family."

"Not much to tell, really. My dad died when I was fifteen. Cancer. My mom about ten years ago. Cancer again. Angie is my only sibling."

"Great job on giving me the facts. Now how about telling me something about them."

"Like what?"

"Like does your sister live in the Portland area?"

"Yeah, somewhere in town. We kind of lost touch when I stopped enabling her drug problem."

She stayed silent for long moments. "That must hurt to know she's close but not be able to see her."

"Honestly?" He glanced at Kat and saw the concern in her eyes making him want to be open with her. "It's harder to see her suffering than not to see her at all. That sounds cruel, but watching someone you love fall apart and realize it's all your fault is tough." He tightened his fingers on the wheel.

"Your fault?"

"After my dad passed away, it was my responsibility to keep the family going. Between my mom's long illness, working to help with the bills and going to school, I missed seeing Angie get involved with the wrong crowd until it was too late."

"That's a whole lot of responsibility for a fifteen-year-old, Mitch. Sounds like you're being a little hard on yourself."

He slowed and eased the car onto his driveway. "You feel the same way about what happened to your mom."

"That's different."

"Seems like the same thing to me." He killed the engine

and shifted to look at her to bring his point home, but before he could continue, he spotted someone sitting on the steps. Just a shadow of a person really.

"There's someone on the stoop." He pointed at his back door. "Stay here and stay alert." He climbed out and drew his weapon as he made his way toward the door.

"About time you got home." The female voice was as familiar as his own.

"Angie?" he said, spotting his sister curled in a ball on the steps.

She was shivering and soaked. Her hair was stringy and her clothes dirty. The same condition as when he'd seen her a year or so ago.

"Why are you here, Angie?" he asked, hating that he sounded so distrustful, but she only stopped by when she needed something.

"I wanna get clean." Her words were slurred.

He sighed and tried to read her expression, but she was high and it was dark. She'd claimed to want to get clean a hundred times before and he'd fallen for it each time.

He should just send her packing, but God help him, he couldn't do it. Not even after all the experts recommended letting her hit rock bottom for her own good. He was going to cave in and let his only living family member come inside and maybe, just maybe, let her tromp all over him again.

Mitch leaned on the wall of his small living room while Princess curled at his feet. He cast a wary eye at Angie as she wolfed down a turkey sandwich and chips. She sat on the sofa next to Kat, who was studying Angie intently. Not that there was much of Angie to see.

She was thin, so thin, but then food took second place to paying for drugs and getting high. Like she was right now. Her eyes glassy. Pupils dilated. Her skin, once soft and peachy, was now sallow and dirty.

His heart broke from the pain. Pain for her. Pain for himself for failing her. Pain for God allowing this.

She finished the last bite of her sandwich. Time to get the show on the road. He went to sit across from her. "So you want to get clean?"

She nodded and took a long drink of her soda, the ice cubes clinking on the glass as her hands trembled.

"Then we should get you checked into rehab."

She leaned back. "Not tonight, man. I need a good night's sleep first."

Here come the excuses. "You can sleep at the clinic."

"Are you kidding? With all the noise in that place?"

"You can't stay here tonight." Mitch tried to sound firm, but he could hear the uncertainty in his tone.

"What? Why not?"

He took Angie's hands. They were cold and clammy. "You know what happened last time we tried this."

"But that won't happen again. I promise, Mitch. I won't do it again."

But she would. Always did. She couldn't resist stealing from him when the craving for drugs got too strong. "I'm sorry, Angie, but either we go to rehab tonight or you hit the road." He cast a quick look at Kat and saw disappointment. That hurt almost as much as this conversation with his sister.

She sank to the floor and put her hands on his knees. The cold penetrated his jeans. How could he send his sister out into weather like this? Only a heartless person could do that. Well, maybe his heart had hardened enough, and he was heartless now.

"Please." She begged not just with her words but also with her eyes like a sad little puppy. "Just one night. I'm only asking for one night." Tears formed in eyes so like his, he couldn't look at her anymore and stay strong.

He rose and crossed the room to get away before he caved. Seeing her reminded him of the months after their dad had died and Mitch comforted her when their mother was too distraught to do so. The days he made sure she had food to eat when their mother was too sick to cook. Nights he'd held her when they were both so lonely for their parents.

Angie came after him and tugged on his arm. "Don't do that, Mitchy. It's me. Your little bug. Remember when you used to call me that?"

He'd never forgotten, but this woman in front of him wasn't his little bug. She was hardly even his sister. "I only have one spare bedroom, and with the way the roads are getting, I think Kat will need to stay there tonight."

"Oh, no, you don't." Kat jumped up. "Don't use me as an excuse to turn her out." She crossed over to Angie and put a protective arm around her shoulder. "If I have to stay, she can share the room with me."

"See," Angie said, her voice hopeful. "Even your friend agrees that I should stay."

Mitch gave Kat a thanks-a-lot glare.

"I'll go take a shower and get cleaned up to give you time to think about it." Angie took off down the hallway, her steps confident and secure. She was biding time because history said if he didn't get her to leave right away, he'd eventually agree to let her stay.

He rubbed a hand over his face as if he could erase the problem. A problem he'd been dealing with on and off for fifteen years now.

Kat stepped in front of him. "You're doing the right thing, Mitch. She needs you."

"What do you know about this?" he snapped out and hated how harsh he sounded. "Your brothers and sister are all decent law-abiding citizens. Not drug addicts waiting to con you out of your house and home if it'll get them their next fix. And then making you feel guilty when you try to stop enabling them."

Kat looked up at him, compassion on her face. "But she said she wants to get clean and she sounds so sincere."

"You were once a cop. How many times did you hear that from junkies on the street?"

"More times than I can count, but this isn't some junkie on the street, Mitch." She paused and held his gaze. "This is your sister."

"Right now, yes, she's my sister. But tomorrow she'll be that junkie again."

"It'll be fine, Mitch." Kat laid a hand on his arm, and the warmth penetrated his sleeve. Maybe his heart. "You should let her stay."

"I want to. Believe me I want to. But…" He let his thought drift off before he made another mistake with Angie.

"I'll help you with her," Kat offered.

"What?"

"Tonight. I'll stay here with the two of you. If there're any problems with her, I'll help in any way you need."

He looked into Kat's sincere gaze, and he couldn't hold out any longer.

"Fine," he said though something inside warned him not to.

Thanks to Kat, his sister could spend the night.

No, that wasn't fair. Even if Kat hadn't been here giving him hope that Angie would change, he still needed to believe she could. The day he stopped believing his sister could return to a normal life, would be a day he'd rather not live to see.

ELEVEN

Kat woke to sun streaming through the bedroom window. Maybe this was a sign that today would be a good day. She looked at her cell phone.

Oh, no.

Her alarm hadn't gone off. She should've gotten up two hours ago. She couldn't believe she'd slept at all, but she had. Deeply. And now she might be too late to go with Mitch to see Nathan's boss.

She jumped out of bed, and hearing low murmurs drifting down the hall, she decided to see what she'd missed. She slipped into her robe and slippers that Dani had tossed in her suitcase yesterday and Mitch had retrieved from his car. She smiled over the memory from last night when a clean Angie had emerged from the bathroom looking more normal. And of Mitch, wrapping those powerful arms around his sister as if welcoming home the prodigal son.

Kat's heart took a leap at his caring—she would never forget the look in his eyes. The softness. The warmth. The love. Maybe because if she searched deep enough inside, she'd admit she wanted him to look at her the same way.

She padded down the hall, her slippers whispering over the wooden floor. She found Mitch alone in the kitchen seated at a round table and talking on the phone.

He turned, his eyes angry and worried at the same time. He put a hand over the phone. "I made coffee. Mugs are in the cupboard above the pot."

She poured a cup, but opted not to join him at the little table. Too small a space for the emotions radiating off him. She leaned against the counter and watched.

He wore jeans again and a dark green shirt, tailored at the waist and emphasizing his broad shoulders. His hair, still damp in the back, curled over the collar.

"Sorry I slept so late," she said when he glanced at her again.

"The roads were too slippery to go out anyway." He met her gaze. "Besides, you needed to sleep."

"And what about you? Did you get any rest?"

He held up a finger and went back to his call. "Are you sure?" he asked, those strong shoulders pulling back as he listened to his caller. "Well, thanks for checking." He hung up and stood, sending the chair crashing into the wall. "Angie's gone. I'd hoped she'd decided to check herself into a clinic but I've called all of them in the area. No one has seen her."

"I'm sorry, Mitch," Kat said, feeling her apology wasn't enough after she'd been the one to convince him to let his sister stay the night.

He shrugged, but the pain remained in his eyes. "It's nothing that hasn't happened before. At least she didn't empty my wallet this time."

"I'm still sorry." Thinking a touch on the arm might help, she took a few steps toward him, but stopped when a shutter dropped over his eyes.

"I made an appointment with Weichert," he said, his voice all business now.

"Did Tommy come through with the warrant yet?"

"Not yet. I'm hoping he'll call before we actually get in to see Weichert."

"We? Does that mean you're not going to argue about me coming with you?"

"No, and I also made sure Cole's fine with you joining me if you want to."

"Yes, of course," she answered quickly and ignored that nagging irritation over the two of them deciding what she could or could not do.

"Good. FYI, the only way Cole agreed to this was if Derrick tails us for added security. You okay with that?"

No, but she nodded agreement or they wouldn't let her make the trip.

"We need to get out of here in thirty minutes if we're going to be on time."

"I'll get ready." With only thirty minutes, she hurried through her shower. She dressed in black pants and a brightly striped shirt that matched the colors of the bruises on her face. With Mitch waiting, she didn't take the time to cover them with makeup, but she would do so in the car. She grabbed her jacket and dropped her cell into her purse, then went back down the hall.

Mitch was still in the kitchen looking at his computer. When she entered the room, he arched a brow. "That was quick."

"You said I had thirty minutes."

"I know I said that, but I really didn't expect you'd do it." He grinned, the smile devastatingly attractive.

"So is that your commentary on women taking too long to get ready?" she asked, liking the change in his mood.

He nodded and came toward her, the smile still in place. He stood toe to toe with her and studied her face before running his finger along her jaw. "Your injuries are healing nicely."

His touch was soft and intimate and words failed her. He bent closer as if he was going to kiss her. She waited for his mouth to descend, instinctively knowing it would be the best kiss of her life. A kiss that spoke of the way they'd connected over the past few days. The way they could connect in the future.

The future. That's what she should be thinking about. Not kissing a man she'd never let into her life.

"We're gonna be late." She backed up and disappointment clouded his eyes, making it even harder to walk away, but she did. She heard him take a deep breath behind her as they walked to the door.

He stepped outside, surveying the area, then giving her clearance to exit. She focused on the glorious sunshine so foreign at this time of year and let the soft breeze chase out the remnants of his touch. They went straight to his car and as Mitch pulled onto the road, they passed Derrick sitting at the curb in his SUV.

They rode silently though the city and nearing their stop, her phone trilled. She opened her purse to retrieve it and found a mess. Someone had rifled through her bag.

Angie? She hoped not.

Mitch had said she hadn't taken his money, but what about hers? She ignored the phone and opened her wallet in the confines of her purse so Mitch couldn't see. No cash. No credit cards. Angie had indeed struck.

How did she tell Mitch about this?

She glanced at him.

"Everything okay?" He smiled warmly at her, and she knew she couldn't tell him how his sister had once again betrayed his trust. Once they got to their appointment, she'd find a way to call and report her credit cards stolen without Mitch overhearing. And that would be the end of this.

"Everything will be just fine," she answered and grabbed her phone to check voice mail. Cole wanted her to know he approved of this outing. He added that he trusted Mitch, but he still wanted to remind her to be careful and not take any chances. Not like Cole at all to be so laid back. He had to have an ulterior motive, but what could it be?

She sighed.

"Problem?" Mitch asked.

"Actually no. Cole just wanted to tell me to be careful."

"So why the big sigh?"

"He has to be up to something. I expected him to grill me about the plans today and insist on accompanying me, but nothing."

"As I mentioned, we worked out the details already so he didn't need to grill you." Mitch smiled, but it lacked any real conviction as he turned back to the road.

He checked the mirrors and his watchful expression reminded her that despite their precautions he was still concerned for her safety. The killer could be waiting for her when she got out of the car. He'd tried to end her life not just once, but three times now and there was no reason to think he'd give up until he completed his mission.

Mitch stood in the reception area outside Weichert's office and watched Kat make a phone call on the other side of the room. She claimed it was too loud with the children and parents chatting near him, but he got the feeling she wanted some privacy.

Not that he minded. He was in a foul mood, and didn't want to take it out on her. He shouldn't let the situation with Angie get to him. After all, he'd expected her to bail again. So why did it always hurt so much?

Without warning, Kat looked at him and instead of being surprised at catching him watching her, she smiled. A soft, intimate smile that he'd wanted to see directed at him. He returned it without thinking of the message he might be transmitting and let the warmth envelop him. She was quite a woman. She'd faced terrible times and came out stronger with her faith intact. She was a role model for him, and he was falling for her. Falling hard.

Is that why You brought us together, Lord?

It was the first time in a long time that he'd even wanted to ask God a question. All because of Kat. Adorable Kat who now crossed the space, her eyes never leaving his.

They were in public—children, parents and staff members milling around—and he only had eyes for her. And she didn't seem to mind. His heart tripped faster. He felt as if he should say something, but what did he say?

I'm falling for you, but I can't do anything about it?

Can't or won't? the uninvited thought popped into his head.

"Detective." Weichert's nasal voice came from behind and Kat's good mood vanished, as did Mitch's.

He signaled for her to follow Weichert who spun on perfectly polished shoes. Her expression as she passed Mitch said she was thankful for the interruption. He was, too, wasn't he?

Weichert stared blankly at them in his office after they all took a seat. "I presume you have your court order."

"Actually," Mitch said, planning to give Weichert an opportunity to confess to his knowledge of the threatening client before he had to drag it out of him. "We have a few questions first."

"What kind of questions?" Weichert crossed his arms leaving Mitch wary. After the morning dealing with Angie's betrayal, he wasn't up for a contentious interview, but it looked like he was about to get one.

"Did Bodig work with a client named Paul, father named Ray?" Mitch asked, forcing neutrality into his tone and watching Weichert for any reaction. A flicker of surprise flashed in his eyes, the response a man with something to hide would have.

"I don't remember a client with that name, but let me check." He turned to his credenza and pecked slowly at his keyboard with one finger. He'd typed much faster yesterday. He was avoiding them. Either stalling for time to come up with a lie about Paul or hiding his emotions so they couldn't tell he was evading them.

Mitch needed to apply a little more pressure. "We're waiting, Weichert."

The man's shoulders tensed, and he hit Enter. "I don't see a Paul."

"How far back are you looking?" Mitch asked, starting to lose patience.

"The last ninety days as you requested on your prior visit." His voice was syrupy sweet, his focus still on the screen.

Despite his frustration, Mitch would give him one more time to come clean before showing him the email and demanding a truthful answer. "And you're certain there's no Paul?"

"I'm certain." Weichert glanced back at him.

"Mind if I take a look?" Mitch slid forward acting as if he intended to take over.

Weichert spun, blocking access to the monitor. "These are sensitive records, and I can't let just anybody view them. Not without that court order."

"Suppose I gave you a court order. Would I see a Paul on the client list?"

"I've already told you there's no client named Paul."

"If that's true, how do you explain this?" Mitch took the evidence bag holding the threat from his jacket pocket and slammed it on the desk.

Weichert picked up the bag and studied the email, his face paling. "This has to be some sort of mistake."

"Then why was it in Bodig's files at his house?" Mitch demanded.

"I don't know." Weichert's voice rose as if he was going to lose it. "I can't explain it."

"Perhaps your report is wrong. Computers aren't infallible," Kat jumped in, her soft tone contrasting nicely with Mitch's harsh demand. Hopefully it would make Weichert finally admit his knowledge of Paul.

"Perhaps," he mumbled.

"Maybe you should check with your staff to see if they know anything about this." Kat smiled, and Weichert relaxed a bit.

"I can do that," he said but stared ahead.

"Now," Mitch commanded.

"Yes, of course." He logged off his computer and hurried out of the office.

Mitch looked at Kat. "I appreciate your giving Weichert the chance to think about this, but it's time we face facts. He's not going to talk without that court order."

"Shouldn't Tommy have gotten that to you by now?" Kat asked.

Mitch dug out his phone and thumbed through his call log just to be sure he hadn't missed one. "Nothing. Worst part now is Weichert knows we're on to him and could destroy records to save his hide."

"You could request an officer to keep an eye on him until we get the order."

Mitch saw Weichert returning so he tipped his head at the door. "I'll give him a stern warning, and we'll see how he reacts before committing any resources to watching him."

Weichert didn't take his chair, but stood by the door and crossed his arms. "No one in the office knows of a Paul and Ray. But I have a few caseworkers out in the field today so I'll follow up with them."

"This is urgent, Weichert," Mitch said.

"I understand. I'll get a hold of them as soon as I can." He smiled, but it was shaky and totally false. "Now, unless you can produce that court order, the weather has messed up our schedules here, and I need to get to work."

Mitch stood and locked gazes with Weichert. "We'll be back with that order. Until then let's be clear on one thing. The email strongly suggests there's a client named Paul in your database and for whatever reason you're not willing to admit it. If you're contemplating destroying records of any kind, that would be grounds for criminal charges. I'm pretty sure you don't want us to file charges against you."

Weichert paled. "No. No. Of course not."

Mitch gave him one last withering look then followed Kat down the hall. "Think we need to send an officer out here?" he asked as they crossed the lobby.

"No."

"Do you have a minute, Detective?" The voice came from behind and Mitch turned to find a short, rotund male hurrying into the lobby from the same door they'd just come through.

"Are you by any chance investigating Nathan Bodig's death?" he asked when he reached them. They nodded in confirmation.

"And you are?" Mitch asked, studying the man.

"George Anderson." He stuck out his chubby hand. "I'm a caseworker here. I worked with Nathan."

"Detective Mitch Elliot and my associate Katherine Justice." They exchanged handshakes.

George took a few steps closer. "I've heard you've been here a few times asking questions about Nathan's cases."

Interesting that he didn't sound sure about this given Weichert's recent questioning of the staff. Maybe he'd just returned to the office.

"Didn't Weichert just talk to you about this?" Mitch asked.

"Weichert? No. I've been swamped with clients at my desk and haven't seen him all morning."

So he had been in the office. Weichert had lied about asking around. Mitch shot a quick look at Kat to make sure she'd caught the significance of this. "Was there something you wanted to tell us about Bodig?"

Anderson glanced nervously over his shoulder. "It's just that...well...I don't think his accident was an accident."

"Why would you think that?" Kat jumped in.

He looked at the office door again then took a step closer. "Just before Nathan's accident the father of one of Nathan's clients went ballistic on him. The boy was killed in juvie and the dad blamed Nathan. He sent threatening emails and even stopped him one night on our way out of work. I thought the guy might punch Nathan, but he settled for poking him in the chest a few times and yelling at him."

"Do you know this father's name?" Mitch asked.

"Ray, but I'm sorry, I don't remember the client's name."

"Did Weichert know about this?" Kat's voice held the enthusiasm Mitch felt in his gut.

Anderson nodded enthusiastically. "Since I was there when the dad went on his rant, Nathan asked me to sit in when he told Weichert." His enthusiasm vanished. "Not that it did any good. The guy blows everything like this off. He says no one's ever been hurt. Now Nathan's dead."

"His death *was* ruled accidental." Mitch didn't want to mislead Anderson in the event that their investigation proved that Bodig's death wasn't intentional.

"I hope so. But I keep thinking it should at least be checked out. You know?"

"I'll be happy to look into it for you," Mitch offered. "Can you get the client's contact information for me?"

One more glance at the door and fear darkened his eyes. "I could lose my job if I do."

"No one needs to know where the information came from," Kat said, ending with a reassuring smile.

"You're certain?"

"Yes." She kept smiling, and Anderson seemed to relax a bit.

"I guess I can get it when Weichert goes to lunch. He always leaves at one o'clock on the nose."

Mitch gave Anderson a business card. "My cell's on the back. Call me the minute you have the records."

"Thank you for being such a good friend to Nathan," Kat added while offering her hand.

"If I had been a good friend, he'd still be alive." Anderson's worried expression returned and he walked away, his shoulders drooping.

"Poor guy," Kat said as she pushed open the door.

"It's not his fault."

"I know." She stopped outside the door and peered up at him. "But then your sister's problem isn't your fault, either, and you still feel responsible for it."

He looked at her then. Her eyes were filled with concern. For him? Maybe. Probably. It warmed his heart and sent it into that funny little spin again, but when he glanced away and caught sight of Derrick sitting guard, Mitch shook off the warm fuzzy feeling and replaced it with hypervigilance.

He might enjoy having her look at him this way, but when she stepped into the open where anyone could attack, his focus needed to be firmly on keeping her alive.

TWELVE

Mitch and Kat arrived at the restaurant where they'd arranged to meet Tommy. He'd called after they'd left Weichert's office, claiming he'd discovered something they'd absolutely want to see. The hostess showed them to a booth, and out of habit, Kat slid in facing the door. Mitch lingered at the edge of the table glancing back and forth to the door before slipping in across from her, a scowl on his face. She should've thought before taking this spot. Cops didn't like to sit with their backs to the door. She didn't, either, but with a family of five who'd worked in law enforcement, she'd had to compromise on that point more times than she could count.

The hostess took their drink orders and Mitch kept glancing over his shoulder and fidgeting with his silverware.

"You want to trade?" she asked, when the hostess left.

He looked at her. "What?"

"Trade sides. So you can face the door."

He smiled, small but real. "That obvious, huh?"

She smiled back at him and patted the bench next to her. "Or you could sit here. I promise not to bite."

He didn't hesitate, but got up and joined her. She felt the heat from his body and instantly regretted inviting him to sit so close. After that intense moment outside Weichert's office when he'd caught her off guard, she didn't want him to think she was doing this because she was interested in him. That would just be leading him on.

"Please promise me you won't try to squeeze Tommy in here, too." He grinned, the crooked little grin that sent her pulse racing.

She laughed and felt all of the day's tension abate. Whatever this was between them, it was good. Really good. Comfortable. And tempting her to want more.

Mitch's cell vibrated on the table, and he seemed reluctant to change his focus to the phone, but he did so, picking it up without identifying the caller.

"Elliot," he said, then listened intently and his smile faded. "What did she do?"

Kat saw him work the muscles in his jaw. Not good news that was for sure.

"Whose credit cards?" His voice shot up, and his gaze swung to Kat, his disappointed look landing on her face and convicting her. She should've thought ahead and known if Angie was arrested for the card use that his fellow officers would give him a heads-up.

"No, I won't bail her out. She can spend the night." He slammed his phone onto the table, his eyes never leaving Kat's. "Why didn't you tell me about your credit cards?" he asked, his voice disturbingly cool.

He was mad. Really mad. She should be concerned about the way he slammed his phone down, but the chill in his voice was far more difficult to deal with.

"I'm sorry, Mitch," she said, though she knew an apology couldn't begin to make up for not telling him. She searched for something to say that would help him understand. "Just think of this like when you called Cole yesterday without telling me."

"That was totally different, Kat. Your life was at stake. I won't die from finding out my sister has pulled another one of her stunts." He watched her with those intense dark eyes, and she didn't look away, but tried to let him see her sincerity.

Taking a risk and putting her hand over his, she said, "You've been through enough. I just didn't want you to be hurt again."

He let out a breath, and his anger faded with it. "I'm sorry I got mad. It's Angie I'm upset with, not you."

"I still should have told you about it."

He lifted his hand still resting under hers and threaded his fingers through hers. "And I should've told you before I called your brother so we're even."

They were back on solid footing—as solid as it could be with the emotions that zinged between them all the time— and she should leave it alone. But she thought he was making a mistake with Angie and she wouldn't ignore it. "Are you sure you want to leave Angie in jail for the night?"

His jaw firmed again. "Once she comes down from whatever drug she's on today, she'll be far more susceptible to the idea of going to rehab where I plan to take her tomorrow."

"I'm no expert on this," she went on, "but if Angie really doesn't want to go to rehab, won't she just check out once you leave?"

"She could, but that's a risk I'm willing to take." That steely shutter she'd seen earlier closed over his eyes and he pulled his hand free, signaling the end of their discussion.

His reluctance to talk reminded her of when she'd arrived at the Justice house and how she'd shut everyone out for months. She didn't resent them for trying to get involved in her life, she'd just never been able to trust anyone with what mattered to her. Maybe Mitch was doing the same thing with Angie. He couldn't trust anyone else to help him and had to go it alone.

The waitress brought their drinks, and when Kat saw

Tommy walk in, she was glad for the company. Plus the sense of urgency on his face said he had a good lead.

"Please tell me you've finally gotten those warrants," Mitch said sullenly before Tommy could sit.

Tommy perched on the edge of the seat across from them. "Not yet. The roads have gotten everything jammed up at the courthouse. But we should have them soon."

"Maybe we'll finally get some answers then," Mitch said, his tone still grim.

"We already have." Tommy pulled out a piece of paper from his pocket and laid it on the table. "I finished going through Bodig's personal files and found this email from his home account. It's generated by a smart phone app. If your phone goes missing and someone plugs it into a USB port on a computer you haven't designated it will send an email alert."

"We use an app like that on our phones at the agency." Kat looked at the email. "Wait. This is dated the day that guy answered Nathan's phone. He must have plugged it into a computer."

"And what good does that do us?" Mitch asked sounding skeptical.

"That, my technophobe partner, is the best part. The email provides the GPS coordinates where the phone was located when it was plugged in."

"So we know where the phone is." Kat couldn't help but be excited about this lead.

"Or was," Tommy said. "The coordinates are for an apartment and you know how fast residents turn over in apartments."

"But at least it's a lead," Kat said, not letting Tommy's comment dampen her excitement. "We need to get over there."

"So much for having lunch for once." Mitch stood and tossed a tip on the table. "I'll pay for the drinks and meet you at the car."

Tommy tugged Kat to her feet. "C'mon, Justice. It's time for you to see two of Portland's finest detectives in action."

Kat rolled her eyes, something she realized she did often around her former partner.

"What's with him?" Tommy nodded at Mitch as he held the door open for her. "You do something to make him cranky again?"

Kat filled Tommy in on Angie's problems on their walk to Mitch's car.

"Really." Tommy eyed her up. "I didn't even know he had a sister."

The thought that Mitch had shared something so personal with her and not with his partner made her heart warm. So did the sight of him as he came out of the restaurant. He had a way of carrying himself with such confidence and it got to her every time.

He gave her a lingering look before opening her car door, and she had to drag her mind off him to where it should be. On the man who was trying to kill her and could be waiting to ambush them when they arrived at his apartment.

The buildings were as run-down as Mitch expected to find in the seedy part of town. He knocked on the manager's door and paint chips fluttered to the ground. He made eye contact with Tommy and silently signaled for him to keep an eye on Kat. He couldn't help but think it was a big mistake bringing her into this neighborhood. Cole would likely have his hide when Derrick told him about it.

The door opened to reveal a stout man wearing a stained T-shirt and baggy jeans. When he saw them, he crossed his arms as if he was itching for a fight. Mitch automatically slid his hand to his weapon.

"Yeah?" the guy asked then scowled.

Mitch showed his badge. "Are you the manager?"

"Super." He fixed wary and distrusting eyes on Mitch.

Mitch's alarm bells clanged so he centered his body in the doorway, blocking escape in case the guy decided to run. "We're looking for information about the resident in apartment 122."

"Alice Leon?" His eyebrows went up in surprise. "What about her?"

"How long has she lived there?" Mitch asked.

He looked up as if thinking. "I dunno. Two, maybe three weeks."

The email from the phone app was dated four weeks ago so she couldn't be the person they were looking for. "And the tenant before her?"

"Ray Granby."

Ray Granby. Mitch glanced at Tommy. His partner's mouth quirked in response as Mitch expected it would. A Ray Granby was wanted for a hit and run of a prosecutor. Detectives in their office were working the case right now.

The super flexed his biceps making the tattoo of a scorpion dance. "That who you're looking for?"

"Could be," Mitch answered. "How long did he live here?"

"Little over two years. Was an okay tenant. Regular payer, anyway. Until his kid died."

Kat's eyes came alive. "He had a son?"

"A teenager. Big troublemaker. Into drugs." He paused and ran the back of his hand under his nose. Mitch had to wonder if the runny nose meant he had some problems with cocaine use himself.

"You know the kid's name?" Kat jumped in, her voice excited.

"Paul." He held up his hand. "And before you ask me what happened to the kid all I know is he got busted and sent up to juvie where someone killed him. Granby really freaked out and went off the deep end. Drinking. Carousing. Finally skipping out owing a month's rent."

"So I take it he didn't leave a forwarding address," Mitch said.

The super laughed. "Even if he didn't stiff me for the rent, we ain't exactly the kind of place where people do that."

"So that's a no then." Tommy sounded as irritated about the guy's attitude as Mitch was getting.

"Anything else?" the super asked, his brow creasing. "My show's on, and I'd like to get back to it."

"That's all." The door slammed almost before Mitch finished his words. "Nice guy, huh?"

Kat lifted her eyes to meet his. "Father Ray, son Paul. Looks like we hit the jackpot."

"About that," Tommy said. "Our department is working on a hit-and-run of a prosecutor and a Ray Granby is the prime suspect. Not sure how long they've been working the case but it seems like a couple of months." He looked at Mitch. "That about right?"

"Give or take a week," Mitch answered, as he turned back to Kat.

"About the same time Nathan died." Kat's eyes lit up. "A caseworker and prosecutor both killed in car accidents around the same. They could've been the ones who got Paul sent to juvie."

Mitch's thought exactly.

"Once we finish up here, I'll call in and see if they can confirm we're dealing with the same guy," Tommy offered.

"I want to talk to Granby's former neighbors before we head out." Mitch tipped his head toward a crumbling sidewalk meandering to the right. "The apartment is that way."

They trekked down the walkway and stopped outside the neighboring apartment. Mitch could hear a baby crying and children screaming on the other side of the door so he pounded loudly.

"What do you want?" a woman's voice came through the cheap wood.

Mitch held up his ID so she could view it through her peephole. "Police. We have a few questions."

The door groaned open and a haggard woman jiggling a fussy baby on her hip gaped at them. Another child, a boy who looked about three, came out and clutched his mother's leg. He wasn't the cleanest, but lacked other signs of neglect.

"Hi there." Kat smiled at the boy, but his little face crumpled in fear and he slipped behind his mother's leg.

"I'm Detective Mitch Elliot." Mitch smiled warmly to ease her concern. "And your name is?"

"Mary," she said and paused as if thinking about what to say. "Mary Brown."

Her evasive look said this wasn't her real name, but he'd play along unless she said something that required him to dig deeper. "Did you know Ray Granby, Mary?"

"You mean the creep who lived next door? Yeah, I knew him."

"Do you know where he lives now?"

"Nah. But good riddance." She moved the baby to the other hip and the child plopped her thumb in her mouth. "After two years of living next to him, we're finally getting some sleep."

"So he was noisy?"

"Noisy, hah! He kept us up all hours of the night. If he wasn't partying he was yelling at his kid and kicking him around."

"You mean hitting him?" Kat's voice rose in disbelief.

Mary shifted the baby again. "Yeah, I guess. I mean I never saw him do it, but the kid always looked pretty rough."

"And you didn't intervene?" Kat sounded resigned to the

fact that there were people who acted this way, but the fire in her eyes said she didn't like it. Not one bit!

"You mean get in between them?" Mary rolled her eyes. "No way I'd cross Ray. He would've gone after me or my kids next."

Kat fisted her hands and glared at Mary. "You are aware that abusing a child is against the law and you're required to report it."

She shrugged as if it wasn't important. "Like I said. I only heard it. Never saw them go at it so there was nothing to report."

"How dare you." Kat took a step toward Mary then stopped as if she knew she could do nothing about it.

Mitch stepped in front of her, and after giving Tommy a look that said take over, he led Kat down the walkway to cool off.

She shook off his hand, but didn't make a move to go back to the woman. "You can't let her get away with that."

"There's not much we can do now, Kat." He waited for her to make eye contact. "Granby's son is dead."

She shoved her hands in her pockets and as she kept glaring at Mary, her breathing grew more agitated. "She should go to jail for ignoring that abuse."

"*If* there was abuse."

"You know there was. And for at least two years if what that woman says is true." Kat shook her head sorrowfully. "This kid might be alive today if someone around here just cared enough to do something."

He was appalled by what Mary said and did, but Kat's reaction ran deeper. She was having a physical response to it, looking like she was going to be sick. He hated to contemplate the source of these emotions but he had to ask. "I can't help but think there's more to your anger than what's going on here."

Her eyes flashed up to meet his and seemed to test him. "Maybe."

"Maybe or yes, Mitch, there's more?"

She studied him more thoroughly, weighing and measuring, then something settled in her eyes and it was as if she knocked down a wall. "She reminds me of my neighbors growing up. They heard my dad yelling and my mom's cries, but pretended everything was okay. Maybe if they cared just a little bit, my mom would still be alive."

"Did your father ever hit you?" He held his breath as he waited for an answer.

"No." She toed her foot into the crumbling concrete, and he relaxed a notch. "There were times I egged him on, hoping he'd leave my mom alone and come after me, but he never did."

Mitch moved closer and circled his arm around her shoulder. "I'm so sorry, honey."

She looked up at him, her eyes awash in pain and at that moment, he wanted nothing more in life than to take away her anguish. To find a way to make up for all those horrible years. To love her the way she deserved to be loved. He just didn't know if he could do it. If he could be the one for her. If she would even let him try.

He heard the apartment door slam and saw Tommy heading their way so he gave her shoulder a quick squeeze and released her.

"Everything okay, here?" Tommy asked, his eyes going first to Kat, then up to Mitch.

Kat took a deep breath and nodded. "You learn anything else?"

"No."

"So on to the next one, then?" She didn't wait for agreement but started off.

Mitch grabbed her elbow. "Why don't we head back to the agency and Tommy'll take care of talking to these people."

Her eyes widened in surprise. "But you said you wanted to do it."

"I know, but I've changed my mind." He turned to Tommy to make sure he understood it was in Kat's best interest to leave this place. "I'll meet you at the office later."

Tommy might be dense sometimes, but he seemed to get what was going on here and he nodded. "Sounds like a plan. Catch you later, Justice," he said, socking her softly on the arm before walking away.

Kat looked up at Mitch, tears starting to form in her eyes. "I'm fine. Really. You didn't have to do this."

"And now I've upset you."

She shook her head.

"Then why the tears?"

"You're just a very nice man, Mitch Elliot. Other than my brothers and Tommy, I don't often run into nice men." She pulled her full lower lip between her teeth and looked up at him with a shyness so foreign to her personality, Mitch's heart took a dip. He couldn't think of anything else but holding her until all of those horrible memories were a thing of the past.

He kept his gaze on hers, and her breath quickened, matching the beating of his heart.

"We should go," she said breathlessly.

He nodded and forced his feet into motion toward the car before he took her in his arms and showed her how much she was starting to mean to him.

THIRTEEN

In the conference room, Kat stood and stretched, her mind going to Mitch. He'd been gone for five hours now, and she missed him. Plain and simple, she'd gotten used to being with him the past few days. He'd called a few times to check in, but it wasn't the same as having him by her side. Worse, she didn't like that he'd put himself on a detail where he could get hurt.

He and Tommy talked with the other detectives and confirmed that the murdered prosecutor had handled Paul's case and Ray Granby had also threatened him. They feared the judge who officiated over the trial was in danger, too. So Mitch and Tommy had gone to check on him and discovered he'd also received a threat from Granby. Now they were sticking close to the judge and running a stakeout to lure Granby out of hiding.

She didn't like not knowing if Mitch was safe. She didn't like it at all. She'd been praying for his safety and for help letting go of the worry, but it still remained in the pit of her stomach.

Enough, Kat. Let it go for now. Keep your mind busy. She went back to Nathan's files that Tommy had dropped off. They may all like Granby for the murder, but they weren't dropping other leads yet.

Cole looked up from his laptop. "You want to see a picture of Granby that Mitch emailed?"

She couldn't bring herself to look at his picture so she checked out the details of his prior arrest records first. He fit the physical profile of the man who'd attacked her and his priors spoke to the violent temper Mary mentioned.

Kat took a deep breath and forced herself to look at him. He had a long face marked by unique scars. If he hadn't worn a mask she could have easily identified him after the attack. His eyes were narrow and untrustworthy. But as much as just looking at him brought back the horrors of her attack, she hadn't a clue if this was the man who tried to kill her.

"Kind of amazing, isn't it," she said, looking at Cole, "that we're looking for the same guy as the other detective team."

"What's amazing to me is that minuscule paint samples are what officially tie the cases together." He closed his computer and leaned back.

She had to agree. The other detectives found an abandoned truck registered to Granby and it not only had a paint transfer that matched the deceased prosecutor's car, but paint from a 2010 Honda. The same year and make of Nathan's wreck. Not conclusive proof that Granby killed Nathan, but strong evidence to add to their case. And now all they needed to do was find and apprehend him. Then once the DNA from her fingernail scrapings came back they'd match it to his DNA, and he'd be on his way to trial.

Only one glitch in this theory. His DNA might not be in the system and they'd have to take a sample from him. That'd take another three days to process. Three more days of this turmoil, and she wasn't sure she could handle that. She sighed.

"Don't worry, Kit Kat. We'll catch this guy." Cole's voice held the iron resolve he was known for. "I promise."

The lights snapped off, the blinding dark sending a chill over her body.

"Cole," she said as that chill intensified.

"Relax," he said, but she could tell by his tone that he was on high alert. "The wind's been blowing all day. Probably just knocked down a line."

"Or not."

"Sit tight. I'll get the flashlight from under the sink."

She heard his slow footfalls as he made his way in the dark across the room. She listened, waiting for any sound out of the ordinary, but she only heard the wind howling outside. Cole could be right. This building was in an older part of town and power lines often went down in high winds.

Cole snapped on the flashlight and shone it her way. "Put on your vest, okay? Just in case."

"Then you do the same." She stood and slipped her vest over her head.

"It's in my office." He crossed over to her, the beam of light dancing ahead of his feet.

"So we'll go to your office and get it then."

"Egress from there is more difficult in case we need to leave the building. It's better to stay here."

"So you don't think this is just the power lines then."

"I'm not sure."

A clicking noise came from the hallway.

"What was that?" she asked.

"Sounds like someone's in the building with us." He grabbed her hand and flipped off the flashlight. "We're getting out of here."

She held her breath as he led her across the room. He stopped at the door and squeezed her hand before letting it go. He drew his weapon, and she did, too.

"Go ahead of me. Back against the wall," he whispered.

"No, I have the vest. You're more exposed so you go first."

He took her hand again and moved her into position. Arguing more would just delay their escape and put them in even more danger. She slid along the wall toward the rear exit. At the stairs, Cole clamped a hand on her shoulder and they stopped.

She listened. Silence. So quiet it was deafening. Then she heard the reason Cole had stopped. Soft but sure footfalls came down the hall behind them. Adrenaline sent her heart racing.

"Go. Now. Outside," Cole whispered urgently. She hurried down the stairs and heard the footfalls running now. At the door, Cole threw it open and shoved her outside. "Take cover."

She ducked behind shrubbery next to the building and waited for him to join her.

A shot split the air, shattering the glass in the door. Flying shards pelted the side of her face feeling like stinging nettles. Cole tumbled outside, his arm red with blood.

"You're hit," she cried.

"It's nothing." He squatted next to her. "Cover me. I'm going for my car."

"No. That'll leave you too exposed."

"Now!" He ignored her request and bolted into the lot.

A gun fired from inside again, the bullet whizzed above her head. She heard Cole rev the engine. Good. He'd made it to the car. She searched for the safest escape route and decided to stay under cover of the shrubs. She slipped along the edge of the building. The car screeched to a stop and the passenger door flew open. She jumped in and Cole floored the gas before she could close the door.

Bullets peppered her side but she managed to get the door closed without being hit as they jerked onto the street, tires squealing. The SUV tipped to the side, and she braced her hand to keep from falling on Cole. They wobbled but finally the vehicle righted itself and they barreled down the street with no one in pursuit.

Cole's shirt was soaked with blood, but his injury wasn't

gushing and didn't look life threatening. Gulping big breaths of air, she reached in the backseat for an emergency kit all the siblings kept in their vehicles.

Her heart rate still elevated, she dug gauze from the kit and opened a package. "You better be heading to the emergency room."

"We'll go to my house. If it's bad enough, I'll head to the E.R. after I find someone to stay with you." Cole alternated his gaze between the rearview mirror and the road ahead.

"Either you go to the E.R., or I'll arrange for an ambulance to meet us at your house." She pressed the gauze against his arm.

He winced. "Fine. But you better get Derrick or Dani to join us or I'll drag you into the exam room with me."

So much for brotherly love. She hated needles and he knew it. "I'll be happy to come in the room with you."

He chuckled, and she felt more of her anxiety and adrenaline rush abate. At least as much as possible under the circumstances. She'd put her brother in the line of fire, the last thing she wanted to do. If only Mitch had been with her instead.

Then what, Kat? That wouldn't be any better now, would it?

She dug out her phone to call Derrick and her finger hovered over Mitch's number instead. She wanted to hear his voice. Just for a second. That's all she'd need. But she might distract him and that could turn deadly on a stakeout so she hit Derrick's icon.

When he answered, she filled him in on the incident. "So if you or Dani could come to the E.R., I'd appreciate it."

"I'll have Dani meet you, and I'll contact the authorities, then head over to the office to secure it." Spoken like a true Justice male. He wanted to protect the women from any hint of danger so he wouldn't let Dani go to the office in case their assailant still hung around.

Kat would normally argue, but she'd be glad to have her sister to talk to at the hospital so she agreed and hung up. She looked at Cole again. His color remained good, there was no fresh blood on the gauze, and he showed no signs of losing consciousness. He would make it. But it had been close. Too close. The very reason she didn't want him or anyone in the family involved in this.

She couldn't lose them. Not a single one of them. And now, even though she hated to admit it, she included Mitch in that group. The big question was, what in the world was she going to do about it?

The family sat around Cole's kitchen table devouring a large pizza with extra cheese just the way Kat liked it. She felt as if they'd gone back to old times. Cole, after leaving the E.R. with a surface wound and bandage matching hers, had called a halt to any talk of the recent events until after they finished eating and it was good just to be with everyone in a relaxed setting.

Almost perfect. Almost. She wanted Mitch here, too. With her family. As part of her family.

The doorbell rang and her gaze flew to the door.

"Relax," Cole said and squeezed her shoulder when he passed behind her. "I doubt the killer has come calling."

He was right. She was becoming paranoid.

"So Ethan will be home tomorrow," Dani said and Kat knew she was trying to distract her from the visitor at the door.

Derrick gave a wry smile. "I'm sure he'll be all over this case, telling us how we've screwed up."

"Where is she?" Mitch's voice rose above their conversation and all eyes in the room turned to her.

"What?" she asked. "I didn't know he was coming."

"No! I need to see her now. Kat! Kat! Where are you?"

He was on the move heading their way and obviously upset about something.

She went to meet him in the living room where the others wouldn't be privy to their conversation. She caught him rushing across the room and was so stunned at the intensity of his worried expression that she stopped in her tracks.

"I heard there was another attack and I was worried about you. Are you okay?" His eyes collided with hers, and she couldn't look away.

"I'm fine," she said, a little breathless from his penetrating study.

"But she's beat and needs to get some rest," Cole said pointedly as he headed for the kitchen. "So don't stay too long."

Kat waited until Cole left the room to speak. "You didn't have to come all the way over here just to check on me, Mitch."

"Yes, I did." His eyes roved from her head to toes and back up again. Then he pulled her close, his fingers threading through her hair and pressing her head against his rock-solid chest. His heart thundered. Hard and fast. Reassuring and unsettling at the same time. "If anything had happened to you I'd—"

His words fell off but she knew what he meant. She slipped her arms around his waist and reveled in the closeness. This felt so good. So comfortable. So right yet so wrong.

"Why didn't you call me?" he asked sounding pained.

"We didn't need your help," she answered truthfully, but purposefully omitted the little detail about wanting to call him.

"Didn't need it, or didn't want it?" he whispered as if it was too painful to say louder.

Neither, she thought. She wanted him near, and God help her, she was starting to need him, too. She leaned back and looked up at him, getting lost in his eyes. She wanted to trust this thing between them, wanted to trust him, but it wasn't that simple after years of being hurt.

Unwilling to lie, but also unwilling to lay her feelings out there as he was doing she said, "Does it really matter, Mitch?"

His eyes clouded over, and he suddenly released her. "If you don't think so then I guess it doesn't."

Her answer had hurt him more than she would've thought. She wanted to take it back, but with the way she wanted to fling her arms around his neck and never let go, getting any closer to him would be a mistake.

"Cole was right," she said. "I'm exhausted and tomorrow's a busy day so I—"

"Should get some rest," he finished for her.

After a long penetrating look that left her unsettled, he headed for the door. With the knob in his hand, he turned and looked at her. "If Angie agrees to go to rehab tomorrow will you go with me to check her in?"

She wanted to say it wasn't a good idea for them to spend any amount of time together for any reason, but the fact that he asked for help with Angie melted any resolve she had to stay away from him. "Yes, of course I'll go."

"I'll call you after I talk to her then." He stepped into the foggy night, and she watched the door close behind him wishing the impossible—that everything keeping them apart would disappear and they could give a relationship an honest chance.

FOURTEEN

Mitch sat in his car. Cold dampness seeped into his body tightening up muscles he'd strained the past few days. His own fault, of course. He could run the heater, but he didn't want the purring motor to alert Kat to the fact that he hadn't been able to leave. She was fine. Safe. Under the watchful eye of her siblings, but he couldn't force himself to turn the key and drive away. Even if she'd just made it clear that she didn't care about him.

Abundantly clear.

His phone trilled in Tommy's ring tone and glad for something to distract him from the aches and pains, he answered it.

"The paint results for your car are back," Tommy said. "The van that ran you off the road is a 2007 Ford. Paint wasn't specific to a model, but we know from your description that it's a full-size van. Ford only made E series vans in '07 so we can search D.M.V. records using that info and the three digits you caught."

"With a logo on the hood, we can assume it's a business van," Mitch offered. "That should narrow it down some."

"Agreed," Tommy answered. "But it'll still be a very long list."

And what amounted to a needle-in-haystack kind of search. Nabbing Granby was still their best option. "So what's happening on the stakeout?"

"We're still a go for Judge Sloan's trip in the morning."

"And you really think after Granby tried to kill Kat tonight he'll switch targets and go after Sloan tomorrow?"

"Sloan seldom leaves town so Granby shouldn't be able to resist the chance to catch the judge—aka me—driving down a country road." Tommy sounded too happy about being Sloan's decoy, and Mitch hoped he'd be careful.

"You want me to be there?" Mitch asked, feeling guilty over not having his partner's back.

"And let you miss slamming that court order on Weichert's desk?" He laughed. "I'll email the vehicle reports to you so you can work on them when you have time." Mitch heard men talking in the background. "Look, I gotta go, but before I do I want to make sure Kat's okay."

"She's fine." At least physically.

"You at Cole's house now?"

"Yeah," Mitch answered though it was only a half-truth.

"Good. I'll catch you tomorrow then."

"Be careful, Tommy," Mitch warned again. "Granby's not someone to mess with."

Mitch hung up and as he was stowing his phone, he saw the front door open and Cole step outside. Even with the thick fog, Mitch could see Cole motioning him to come inside. He knew it wasn't a good idea to go anywhere near Kat tonight with everything in turmoil between them, nevertheless he climbed out and on legs stiff from the cold, made his way up the walk.

"You planning on spending the entire night out here?" Cole asked, an eyebrow rising.

"Yes."

"She's safe with us, you know."

"I know."

"But you can't leave."

"Something like that."

"Look, Elliot," Cole widened his stance. "You seem like a stand-up guy and could be good for Kat, but I have to warn you, she'll break your heart."

"You sound pretty sure of that."

"Sometimes I think there's nothing in this world that'll get her to let go of her past and trust a guy." Cole pushed open the door, but caught Mitch's gaze before stepping back. "She wants to talk to you, but if you hurt her, I'll make you pay."

Great. Not only did Cole tell him that it'd be impossible for Kat to let go of her past enough to trust him, but if she got hurt in the process, a man who Mitch wouldn't want to tangle with would hunt him down and make him pay. Made Mitch want to run the other way, but staying here tonight was as important as breathing to him so he stepped inside.

Warm air instantly started thawing his face, but Kat's chilly eyes sent him back to the deep freeze. He crossed the room to where she stood in front of a fireplace ablaze with a roaring fire. He was vaguely aware of Cole passing through the room, but Mitch couldn't take his eyes off Kat. "You wanted to see me?"

"Why are you still here?" It sounded like an accusation.

"I'm in charge of this case, and I don't want anything bad to happen on my watch."

A delicate eyebrow arched. "You're just here doing your duty, nothing else?"

He wouldn't put his feelings out there to be trampled on again either. "Mostly, yeah."

She looked at him then, long and hard, and he couldn't have looked away if he'd wanted to. "I don't need you to stay, Mitch. I'm a big girl."

"Lori used to tell me that all the time, too." He'd failed to protect her and now he was all alone. A slice of loneliness caught him off guard and he wanted to say more. There'd been no one else to challenge his memory of Lori. To make him want to let go and move on. Until now. Until Kat.

"I'm not Lori," Kat said, her tone still cool.

"No, but when you shut me out it makes me feel helpless like I did when she rushed ahead of me that day." He shook his head. "Let me help, Kat. Please. I need to help."

She appraised him for long silent moments and something changed in her eyes. As if she finally accepted him or at least accepted his insane need to be in charge. "I won't have you sitting in your car all night. I'll get bedding for the couch." She walked away, and he let out a breath.

They'd made progress. What kind of progress, he didn't know. But at least he would be here if she needed him. Not that she would. She'd rather die than admit she needed him. Just like Lori. Strong and independent. But that's where the similarities ended.

Lori was sunshine and rainbows, keeping him on the right path. Kat was a bulldog, all thunderclouds and lightning, with a past that made her tough and wise. But also closed, with a wall so high, Cole might be right. Maybe it couldn't be knocked down.

She came back, her head barely visible above a pile of bedding. She navigated her way to the sofa, then dropped the linens and turned to leave.

He couldn't let her walk away. He'd probably regret it, but he reached for her hand and pulled her close. "I know you're capable, Kat, and I'm sorry if I keep pushing your comfort zone. But you're starting to mean too much for me to take any chances."

His admission seemed to catch her by surprise for a moment, but then she smiled up at him, the first time in days when she'd looked at him as she had in the past. He waited for her to walk away but she stood there, her eyes on his. Alive and real. So much better than simply settling for memories of a relationship in the past as he'd done since Lori died.

He wanted to touch her. To kiss her. But he shouldn't. He hesitated for a moment, waiting for her to bolt. But when she didn't he caved, running his fingers gently over her cheek. She shivered and a spark ignited in her eyes. His nerves fired in a chain reaction. There was a connection here, beyond anything he'd felt before, and no matter the consequences, he was going to kiss her.

He lowered his head, waiting for her to protest, but when she didn't he swooped in and claimed her mouth. Her lips were soft and warm, sweeter than he could have imagined. He dragged her into his arms and deepened the kiss.

Don't do this, his brain shouted. *You're not ready for this. You'll only hurt her and she deserves more than that.* He started to lift his head, but she twined her arms around his neck, holding him in place and returning his kiss.

"Did you find the bedding?" Cole's voice came from behind them and slowly worked its way into Mitch's muddled brain.

He lifted his head, fearful of the expression he might find on Kat's face. But she smiled again, this time knowingly, and those nerves fired again.

"Go away, Cole," she said, making no move to break out of Mitch's hold.

"I guess this means you found everything you needed," Cole's tone held humor, but as his gaze connected with Mitch's he saw a note of warning, reminding him of their conversation outside and bringing him back to reality.

This was exactly what Mitch didn't want to happen. To start something he wasn't sure he could follow through on. He needed to have a talk with her. To get things out in the open before kissing her again.

He drew her arms from his neck and stepped back. "I shouldn't have kissed you, Kat."

The interest in her eyes quickly extinguished and went cool. Then cold. Ice cold. "You're right. This was a mistake. Good night, Mitch." She turned and walked away.

He wanted to reach out for her. To stop her and insist they talk about this. But maybe it was better to let their emotions cool down and have their discussion in the light of day when they weren't so tired.

Yeah, that was the right thing to do. So if it was right then why did watching her walk away hurt so badly?

Hours later, Kat went to the guest bedroom door and listened. Silence. Everyone had gone to sleep except her. She was too hyped up to even attempt to sleep. She'd tried to read for hours. The words all blurred together, and she kept thinking about Mitch. He was right; they shouldn't have kissed.

Not because she didn't want to kiss him. She did. Again and again. She knew that now. Knew it with a certainty, but she'd also figured out why he kept pulling back. He wasn't over losing Lori, and he'd mixed up all those feelings about her with caring for Kat. Knowing that should make her feel better, but it didn't.

How could she when she was a stand-in for another woman?

She needed a cup of tea to help her relax if she was going to get any sleep. She kicked off her slippers so as she went through the family room she wouldn't make noise and wake him up. As she passed the sofa, she imagined him asleep, his guard down, looking vulnerable. With a silent groan over her traitorous thoughts, she hurried on and crashed into a small table, sending it wobbling.

Mitch leaped up, his gun drawn.

She jumped back. "Relax. It's just me."

"Kat?" he asked, his voice low and gruff.

"Yeah, who'd you think it would be?"

He whooshed out a breath and switched on a lamp. He still wore his jeans, but had shed his shirt and a white T-shirt hugged his body. "Don't you know better than to sneak around a house filled with people who own guns?"

"I didn't want to wake you."

"I wasn't sleeping." For some reason his admission gave her hope again. Hope that maybe he wasn't confused about Lori, but he'd lain awake thinking about her. Hope that the caring she'd seen in his eyes earlier really was just for her.

She tipped her head at the kitchen. "I'm going to make some tea. You want some?"

He watched her for a long moment, then shook his head. "But I'll sit with you while you make it."

She heard his bare feet hitting the wood floor behind her on the way to the kitchen. She grabbed the teakettle and filled it with water.

He took a stool across the island from her. "I'm sorry, Kat."

Surprised at his statement, she spun. "For what? Kissing me?"

"No. I shouldn't have done that, but I'm not sorry I did." He let his gaze linger until she felt her face color. He came around the island and stood facing her. "What I'm apologizing for is barging in here tonight. Your family can take care of you. You don't need me."

She did need him. That was now clear. But with all the turmoil between them, she wouldn't tell him. "It's okay, Mitch. I get it. Taking care of me is your way of working through losing Lori."

"That's part of it, I guess." He slipped a strand of hair behind her ear, and she had to work hard to concentrate on what he was saying.

"And the other part?"

"I like spending time with you. When you're not with me, I miss you." He smiled and the warmth of it had echoed in his words.

"I like spending time with you, too," she admitted and found it impossible not to return his disarming smile.

He suddenly laughed. "I just never knew I'd have to battle your brother to get close enough to talk to you."

"Who, Cole?" she asked and he nodded. "You'd do the same thing for Angie if she was in this situation."

It was almost as if she threw a wet blanket over his head as his eyes darkened. "And more, I guess. Problem is I can't help her."

"Hopefully she'll agree to go to rehab tomorrow."

"I'm guessing she will, but what you said earlier is probably true. I'm the one pressing her to go. She has to want to do this on her own or she won't stay in the program."

"Still it's a start, right?"

The teakettle whistled, and she turned away.

He reached out and caught her hand, giving it a squeeze. "Tomorrow's going to be a long day. We should get some sleep." He walked away and though she was tempted to watch him, the teakettle demanded her attention.

She went to the stove and prepared a cup of chamomile. Probably the first of many because she knew without a doubt she'd spend the night remembering his gentle touch and not get a wink of sleep.

FIFTEEN

Outside the rehab center the next morning, tears glistened in Angie's eyes while she hugged her brother. As she pushed out of Mitch's arms, Kat could barely keep her own tears at bay as she watched them say goodbye.

"It'll be okay, bug," he said, then took a few steps back. "I'll come visit as soon as I'm allowed."

Kat was touched at his use of his sister's nickname, and if Angie's tears flowing over sunken cheeks were an indication, so was she.

Mitch reached up as if to wipe them away, but then seemed to think better of it and shoved his hands in his pockets. Tears continued to prick Kat's eyes. For Angie, yes, but mostly for the anguish on Mitch's face. On the thirty-minute drive, Angie was sweating, shaking and huddled in a ball, not aware of what was going on, but Kat saw Mitch white-knuckle the steering wheel for the entire ride. He'd acted so tough so strong and optimistic for Angie, but he was hurting. Badly hurting.

Angie turned to Kat and Mitch backed even farther away. "Thanks for keeping Mitch company on the ride."

Kat dug out one of her business cards and pressed it into Angie's palm. "Feel free to call me if you need something and can't get a hold of Mitch."

Angie flung her arms around Kat's neck. "Please make sure he's okay once you get on the road," she whispered. "I love him so much, and I've done nothing but hurt him."

"I will," Kat answered earnestly, but she wasn't sure how she could help him or even if he'd let her.

Angie leaned back. "You love him, too, don't you?" she said so quietly Mitch couldn't possibly have heard.

Kat nodded. "Don't worry about Mitch. I'll take care of him, Angie."

Angie gave a clipped nod and after a long look at her brother, she rushed away.

Kat took a few deep breaths and joined Mitch as he stood looking over the peaceful rolling hills of the property just outside the Portland metro area. The lush green landscape belied the harsh struggles of people inside this facility.

"Weichert is expecting us." He gestured at his car, his iron control back in place. Jaw tight. Mouth a flat line. Shoulders rigid. And she wanted to smooth it all away. To tell him things would be okay. But would they? Would Angie stay here? The odds were against her.

They went to his car and, ever the gentleman, he opened her door and made sure she was seated before climbing behind the wheel.

"She'll be okay," Kat said, sounding so lame and wishing she could've thought of something better to say.

He didn't respond as he eased the car out of the parking lot and onto the main road.

"Not that I've gotten very good at this yet, but I know it would be a lot easier on you if you could leave this in God's hands," Kat said. "Would you like me to pray for her?"

"Please."

Kat took his hand from where he rested it on the gearshift and twined her fingers with his. He glanced at her and his gaze held such tenderness that she had to draw in a deep breath before offering a prayer on Angie's behalf. She finished her plea then squeezed his hand. She expected him to pull it free, but he didn't move.

"For the first time in a long time, I feel like that really might help," he said and smiled at her. "Thanks to you."

She squeezed again, and he lifted her hand to his lips where he pressed a soft kiss before letting his hand settle on his knee, hers still held firmly by his.

She should be thinking about their upcoming meeting with Weichert but thoughts about the wonderful man sitting next to her filled her mind. She took a quick look at their hands twined together and knew if she wanted to be happy, it was time for her let go of her past.

To let God take charge. Once and for all, really let Him take charge.

To trust Him no matter what happened and start living again.

To live as she had before the fear of loss took over and maybe, just maybe, find that contentment that had been so elusive in her life.

"All right. Fine," Weichert grumbled from behind his desk. "I knew about the letter. Knew about it, but didn't do anything. So yeah, it's my fault Nathan was killed. When my supervisor finds out, he'll fire me. That's why I had to cover it up."

Mitch actually felt sorry for the man, but he'd still have to pay for his mistakes. "Is there a reason you ignored the letter?"

"We get threats all the time, but no one ever follows through on them. I thought this was just another one of those and we're so overworked here that I didn't want to take the time to check it out."

Mitch's phone chimed Tommy's ring tone. "Now would

be a good time to start making up for stonewalling us and make a copy of Paul Granby's file," Mitch said as he dug out his phone. He was liking Granby for the attack, but he still needed to cover all bases so he added, "And I'd also like that list of Bodig's coworkers, too."

Weichert hopped up and rushed out of the room.

Mitch answered his phone and put it on speaker for Kat.

"We got him," Tommy's excited reply came through the speaker.

"What?" Kat asked.

"Granby. We arrested him." The excitement in Tommy's voice said he was still on an adrenaline high.

"Good job, partner," Mitch said and watched Kat for her reaction. She seemed pleased but something else lurked in her eyes.

"We'd like you to come down to the station, Kat," Tommy went on. "I've arranged an auditory lineup. I'm hoping you can recognize Granby's voice and ID him as the man who attacked you."

Kat visibly recoiled from the phone, her eyes filling with dread. Mitch had seen the same look in other victims' eyes when they'd been called upon to see their attacker again and all the memories of their assaults came flooding back.

"Kat," Mitch said so she'd focus on him, not on her fears. "He's in custody. He can't hurt you."

"I know," she replied, and yet she still shivered.

"Tommy and I'll both be with you."

"In an official capacity, of course," Tommy said, making her cringe again.

"Once we finish with Weichert, we'll be down there." Mitch clicked off his phone before Tommy could say anything else to make this worse for Kat.

"It's okay, Mitch. I know you'll both have to keep a professional distance at the lineup." She sounded so sad, as if she'd lost her best friends.

In a way, she had. Granby's lawyer, if he'd requested one, would be in the room with Kat and if he caught even an iota of personal involvement between any of them, it could jeopardize the case.

Never had Mitch been so torn between his job and his personal life.

Weichert came back into the room and handed over a thick file. "If you need anything else, please call."

Mitch noted the change in attitude, but they wouldn't likely need anything else from this man. In fact, after Granby's arrest they probably didn't even need the file or the employee list, either. Still, he'd take it to be able to insure the man who'd sent this amazing woman next to him running in fear spent his life behind bars.

Mitch urged her to her feet and escorted her to the car, passing Derrick who sat in his vehicle again today. Mitch could tell Derrick to go home, but until Mitch physically saw Granby in handcuffs, he wouldn't relax a bit.

Kat settled in and immediately opened Paul's file as if she wanted to take her mind off the upcoming lineup. Mitch knew it would be better if she talked about it, but he wouldn't force her to. Still he didn't want her to feel alone. So he took her hand and wordlessly slipped his fingers through hers again.

She glanced up at him, her tender expression saying he'd done the right thing by supporting her silently.

Good. He only hoped he could figure out how to do the same thing without touching her when she relived every horrifying moment of her attack, moment by moment, as she identified the man who'd tried to kill her.

The minute they entered the Justice Center in downtown Portland Kat felt Mitch withdraw behind the professionalism of his shield. She got that he had to step back from her, though she didn't like it. But she could look at it positively. With Tommy keeping his distance, too, now was the perfect time to put all of her trust in God.

They rode the elevator to the thirteenth floor, her stomach burning with acid. When the doors slid open, she saw Tommy standing near the secured door to the department. They joined him, and Mitch congratulated Tommy on his collar of Granby with a fist bump.

"You interrogate him yet?" Kat asked, hoping he'd say Granby confessed to killing Nancy, and she wouldn't have to see the man until his trial.

Tommy nodded. "He's not saying much. Lawyered up right away. But you'll be happy to know he doesn't have an alibi for the night Nancy was murdered, and he has scratches on his arm consistent with your assault. Plus we confiscated a variety of drugs from his vehicle, which gives us reason to believe he had access to propofol."

"That's good then." Kat wanted to smile, but the thought of the man who'd attacked her sitting in this building—so close she could almost feel him—made her stomach churn even more.

"What was he driving?" Mitch asked.

"A stolen pickup," Tommy answered. "We figure he knew we had an alert out on the van and ditched it. Hopefully a patrol officer will come across it and that'll help solidify our case."

"Did you collect any other forensic evidence?" Mitch asked.

"Granby's DNA isn't in the database, so we swabbed him. I'm expecting it will come back as a match to Kat's fingernail scrapings." Tommy put a hand on Kat's shoulder. "Ready to do this?"

She nodded, though her stomach was still in knots. Tommy

slid his card through the card reader and pressed her forward with gentle pressure on her back. At the end of a long hallway, they went into a small room with a one-way mirror.

"You know the drill," Tommy said. "Since you've seen a photo of Granby we have the men in ski masks similar to the one you described. Each one will read a specific phrase and all you need to do is listen and let us know if you recognize his voice." He nestled an arm around her shoulder and squeezed. "Okay?"

"Okay."

Mitch stood stoically next to her, and she wished he could take her hand.

"Here we go." Tommy pressed an intercom button on the wall. "Send them in."

Kat squared her shoulders and watched as six men, all about the same size and build, filed into a room.

"Number one, read your phrase," Tommy instructed though the intercom.

"Nancy had no right to share this information with a private investigator," the man said. "Your death is her fault, not mine."

Terror hit Kat hard, and she stepped back.

The words were so similar to the ones said by Nancy's killer that Kat flashed backed to that night. She felt arms of steel holding her down. Saw the anger in his eyes, the thin line of his mouth as he held the syringe. Her heart started racing, and she glanced at Tommy.

"How did you know what to have him say?" The words came out in a whisper, telling them both how unsettled she was.

Mitch turned his back to the lawyer and met her gaze. She could feel the tension radiating off him, but his eyes were tender. "You told me the night of the attack so it's in our notes."

Her heart pounded harder, and her legs trembled so she braced her hands on the back of a chair.

Help me, Father, she begged and took deep breaths sending out the anxiety with each exhale. She could tough this out. After days of uncertainly, it was almost over now. She wouldn't back down.

"Have him repeat it, Tommy," she said and closed her eyes to listen more carefully.

She felt Mitch move behind her. He stood close and warmth radiated from his body. He didn't touch her, but he was telling her that he was there for her. He was supporting her. With God above and Mitch close by, she would not back down.

"Nancy had no right to share this information with a private investigator. Your death is her fault, not mine." The line was repeated over and over, her eyes scrunched closed listening as if her life depended on it. Tommy occasionally asked the suspect to speak clearer and louder until the last man said his line and her heart sank. She couldn't identify any of them.

"Well?" Tommy asked and she opened her eyes already filling with ears.

"I wish I could say it was one of them, but I'm just not sure." She looked up to stem the tears. "I'm so sorry, Tommy."

"It's okay, Kat," Mitch said softly, still standing behind her.

"But I was a cop. I know how important it is to pay attention to details. I should be able to do this."

"Cut yourself some slack, Kat," Tommy said. "You were fighting for your life that night. Details take second place to staying alive."

She heard the conviction behind his words, but the disappointment in his eyes said she'd failed. And she had. Big time. She was the only connection between this creep and Nancy's death. Until the DNA came back. That would prove his part in all of this. At least she hoped it would because she couldn't stomach the thought that her failure to identify Granby would allow a killer to go free.

SIXTEEN

Mitch walked Kat to the door of her town house. He didn't like the idea of her staying home alone, but with Granby behind bars, she was safe. Finally, safe.

She slipped her key into the lock, and he tried to come up with a reason not to leave. He had no logical reason to stay, but he just plain didn't like the idea of her not needing him anymore.

Even worse, he didn't like the idea of her needing him in the future and failing to be there for her. This afternoon's lineup reminded him of how easily she could be hurt, perhaps killed. He hadn't been there for her the night a man had beaten her. Tried to kill her. The odds of that happening again were slim, but it could happen again. Especially working for the agency.

She pushed open the door and turned to him. "Thank you for bringing me home. And for everything you've done the past few days. I couldn't have gotten through it without you."

He felt the sincerity in her words, but he couldn't look in her eyes without blurting out something he wasn't ready to admit to himself, much less to her, so he peered over her shoulder, searching for a reason to stay. He may not be ready to commit to anything with her, but he still didn't want to leave her alone.

He saw the mess left behind when the F.E.D. team processed her place for fingerprints and other forensic evidence. He tipped his head toward the disarray. "How about you put on a pot of coffee, and I'll help you clean up from F.E.D.?"

She turned and looked at her room, not speaking, not moving. He had no idea what was racing through her very complicated mind, but he wouldn't wait for her to say no. With a gentle hand on her shoulder, he urged her inside.

"Do you want me to make the coffee?" he asked while helping her out of her jacket.

She peered up at him. She looked lost and adrift, but she gave a firm shake of her head. "I can do it."

"I'll get started cleaning up the fingerprint powder if you tell me where you keep your vacuum."

"In the laundry room in the hall." She went to the kitchen, and he settled their jackets over a chair, then went to retrieve the vacuum.

She seemed distant, almost robotic, and he wanted to make sure she was okay. So he waited until he heard the coffee grinder come alive before firing up the vacuum. He mounted the hose on the body and after figuring out how to change the settings, he circled the room sucking up the powdery substance.

Expecting Kat to join him, he kept glancing at the kitchen. When he was certain the coffee had to be done, he flipped off the switch and went to the kitchen. She stood, her back to him, her forehead resting against a stainless refrigerator. Her shoulders shook, and his heart plummeted to his feet.

He went to her and gently drew her away from the refrigerator and into his arms.

"Shh, Kat. It's okay." Her soft crying turned heavy, her body heaving as he stroked her back and urged her to calm down. "Everything's okay," he kept whispering until her sobbing slowed.

He rested his chin on her head and held it against his chest where he was certain it belonged. Not just now, but whenever she needed him. He wanted to be there for her.

Always.

Forever.

The startling thought jerked his head up. She must have sensed the change in him as she pushed back, freeing herself from his arms.

She grabbed a tissue from her purse on the counter. "Sorry about that." She dabbed at her eyes. "I've been holding it all in since Nancy died and the dam finally burst." She gave a nervous laugh. "I bet you wished you'd left me at the door."

He didn't wish that at all, but something inside kept him from answering. From letting her know how he felt. He nodded at the coffeepot. "Mind if I have a cup while I clean?"

She took a step back as if he'd physically wounded her and then forced a smile.

"Help yourself." She squatted down by the cabinet under the sink and pulled out cleaning supplies while he poured his coffee.

They were back to polite strangers. What he wanted, right? So why did he feel so empty inside?

In the spare bedroom, Kat waited for Mitch to turn off the vacuum. They'd shared a tender moment in the kitchen, and she was certain a strong bond existed between them that could take them beyond tonight. She'd tried to broach the subject several times. He'd shut her down by firing up the vacuum and turning away, but this was too important to give up on.

So she'd try one more time.

He flipped the switch and hit the button to retract the cord. "Well, that's it then. All clean."

"Mitch," she said and walked over to him.

He looked at his watch. "Wow, look how late it's getting.

You need some rest." He lifted the vacuum and didn't make eye contact. "I'll just put this in the closet and be on my way."

She followed him downstairs, her anger at his behavior mounting with each step. But why was she surprised at how he was acting? This was exactly what she'd feared, wasn't it?

Mitch in control. Deciding how and what they would do. Deciding if she could speak to him or not. Cold and withdrawn. Calling all the shots. Still too hampered by his fear of losing Lori to risk a new relationship.

He grabbed his jacket from the back of the chair and looked her in the eye for the first time since they'd left the kitchen. "Make sure you lock up after me," he said, and she saw his sincere concern for her well-being in his gaze, softening her anger a bit.

"I will," she answered and joined him at the door.

He opened it and stood for a moment, looking down on her. The concern changed to longing but just as fast vanished leaving the hard resolve she'd seen years ago when he'd rejected her. She couldn't look at him so she stared at his chest.

"I'll let you know when the DNA results are back." With a gentle finger, he tipped her chin up and planted a kiss on her forehead. Chaste and brotherly. Not at all what she was feeling.

He stepped outside and closed the door. She looked around the room. Spotless thanks to him and she suddenly couldn't be alone so she called Dani.

When her sister answered, tears starting flowing and she could hardly get out her request for company.

"I'm just down the street," Dani said. "I'll be there in three minutes flat."

Kat leaned against the door and waited. If Dani said three minutes, she meant it. No one was as prompt as her sister. Kat soon heard the gentle clip of Dani's feet coming up the walk so she pulled open the door.

Dani shoved a container of cookies into Kat's hands. "I was on my way to take these to Cole, but you need them more."

Kat opened the container and inhaled the warm chocolate scent. "You're a lifesaver."

Dani slipped out of her jacket and went to the sofa. "So tell me all about it."

"Let me get some coffee to go with these first." Kat set the cookies on the table and went to pour what remained of the pot she'd made for Mitch.

Kat handed a cup to Dani, then settled next to her and described what had just transpired with Mitch. When she finished, she took a cookie, raised it in salute, then chomped into it, savoring the way the chocolate was still warm and gooey.

She moaned and chased the bite with a sip of coffee. "I'm feeling better already."

Dani rolled her eyes. "You can't keep ignoring this thing with Mitch by eating cookies."

"Agreed, but what else can I do? He made it clear that he didn't want to talk about us. Hah! Us. There is no 'us.' Just wishful thinking on my part."

"Do you really believe that?" Dani looked at her over the rim of her cup.

Did she?

"I mean, you're a smart woman," Dani went on. "If you think there's something between the two of you then there is."

"So what if there is?" Kat sighed. "This just isn't the right time for either of us."

Dani snorted. "Puh-lease. It's not about timing and you know it. We all agree he's into you."

"What?" Kat said, nearly choking on her cookie. "You guys talked about us?"

Dani rolled her eyes again. "There's nothing off-limits in our family and you know it."

"I know, but sometimes I'd rather forget it."

Dani swatted Kat's knee. "Quit trying to get us off track. Your solution is really simple. Mitch is holding back and once you figure out why, your problem is solved."

It wasn't as simple as Dani made out. Kat knew why he was holding back. Knew it well, but wouldn't share something so personal with Dani. Plus there was no point in really talking about his fear of failing the woman he loved because there was nothing she could do about it. Only God could work on Mitch's heart and that thought made Kat sadder than she'd been in a long while.

Two days later, Mitch sat back and glanced around the nearly deserted homicide division. In the three hours he'd bent over his desk looking at paperwork for a new case, his fellow detectives had called it a day. So should he. But he'd phoned the lab to check on Granby's DNA and was told the report would be on his desk that day. So when Tommy asked him if he wanted to grab a bite for dinner, Mitch made up an excuse to hang around the office and wait for the report.

Not because he really thought it would hold anything surprising, but having the results in hand would give him a reason to go see Kat after two days of trying to come up with a legitimate reason to talk to her.

The door opened and Cole Justice strode in. Surprising. Not just because it was Cole, but because they worked in a secured area and Cole would have had to jump through hoops to get in here.

"Working kind of late, aren't you, Elliot?" He stopped in front of Mitch's desk.

Mitch leaned all the way back in his chair and clasped his hands behind his head. Though Cole had called once a day to ask about the DNA, Mitch hadn't seen him or any of the Justices in two days. And the scowl on Cole's face said he wasn't here for a social visit.

"What can I do for you, Cole?" Mitch asked warily.

Cole raised a brow, probably from Mitch's testy tone. "Just checking in to see if that DNA report has come in yet."

"You could've just called again," Mitch said wryly.

"I could've." Cole dropped onto the chair next to Mitch's desk.

"So why're you really here?" Mitch asked.

Cole leaned forward, his expression unreadable. "Haven't seen you around the past few days."

Great. Could they dance around things or what? "With Granby's arrest, I haven't had a reason to be around."

Cole fixed a stare on Mitch. "Why're you avoiding Kat?"

If Mitch wasn't a confident man, he'd wilt under Cole's scrutiny, but this was none of Cole's business so Mitch didn't respond.

"I'm pretty sure I told you what I'd do if you hurt her." Cole sat up his back ramrod straight, and his eyes narrowed.

Mitch wanted to deny hurting her, but he knew he had. Their last night together, she'd repeatedly tried to talk to him, to get him to open up, and he'd shut her down every time. Then, she'd walked him to the door, and he'd left her with such aching pain in her eyes. It was all he could think about for the past two days.

"Fine," Cole said. "You don't need to explain it to me. But you do need to talk to Kat. Anything else is unacceptable." Cole held Mitch's gaze.

Cole was right. Mitch did need to have a conversation with Kat. For her and for him. Officially ending what hadn't yet begun was the only way he was going to get her out of his mind. "I'll give her a call and set something up."

"See that you do." Cole leveled that firm gaze on him again.

Not wanting to feel even more like a cad for not talking with Kat, Mitch looked away and caught sight of the door opening again. He watched a tall man dressed in a pricey suit enter the room and look around before approaching them.

"Is one of you Elliot?" he asked, his voice deep and rumbling.

"Who's asking?" Mitch's response came out testy from his conversation with Cole.

"Special Agent Larry Reed." The man held out an official-looking ID.

Mitch confirmed it was a legitimate FBI credential, then turned to Cole. "If you'll excuse us."

Cole rose, and Reed offered him an apologetic look. "Sorry to stop by this late in the day, but I was hoping to close out a case involving Nancy Bodig."

"What about Nancy Bodig?" Cole asked before Mitch could say anything.

Reed raised a brow. "You working the Bodig case, too?"

"Yes," Cole answered.

Mitch didn't want to go into a lengthy explanation of Cole's involvement, so he asked Reed, "Nancy Bodig?"

"Right," Reed answered. "We've been investigating money laundering at a local business and her name came up today."

Money laundering? Mitch didn't believe it. If she was involved, they would've found something in her bank records or in her spending habits. "We fully vetted her and there was nothing to suggest money laundering."

Reed stared at Mitch. "Perhaps you'd like to hear me out before dismissing this so quickly."

"I definitely want to hear it." Cole plopped back down and crossed massive arms across his chest.

Mitch glared at him, but knew nothing short of physically throwing Cole out would get him to leave, so Mitch grabbed the side chair by Tommy's desk for Reed before sitting behind his own desk. The agent turned the chair around and straddled it. Mitch recognized this for a Mr. Tough Guy routine feds often pulled to prove they were in charge, but there was no point in saying anything about it.

"Norton Construction has been under suspicion for years for their ties to local drug dealers," Reed finally said. "But we could never get anything on them. Today, the receptionist, an Alisha Walters, told us that the owner Jesse Norton was keeping two sets of books."

"What made Walters turn on him?" Mitch asked.

Reed shifted in the chair. "When Walters first worked for the company she didn't know what Norton was up to. Then she got involved with him, started hanging around more and noticed his illegal activities. She claims when she discovered what he was up to she wanted to break things off, but with all she knew about Norton's activities, he'd come after her. So she waited for a way out. When she discovered she was pregnant she had to get out before Norton found out about the kid."

"And that's when she came to you?" Mitch asked.

"No. She figured if law enforcement got involved she'd have to testify against Norton."

"And she was afraid he'd kill her," Cole said.

"Exactly. So she hatched her own plan and that's where Bodig came in. Walters knew Bodig only had access to the legit set of books. So Walters made sure records from the illegal activities were left where Bodig would pick them up on her weekly visit. Since Bodig was a churchgoer, Walters figured once Bodig got a look at this info, she'd report Norton to the authorities."

"So what went wrong?" Mitch asked, not liking where this was heading.

"Walters didn't know Norton had the office under video surveillance, and he saw Bodig take the books. When we heard Bodig had been murdered—"

"You figured Norton took her out," Cole interrupted, his worried gaze going to Mitch's.

"This Norton Construction company have a logo?" Mitch asked and held his breath waiting for the answer.

"Yeah. A black circle with the word Norton in red letters. Why?"

Mitch felt the blood drain from his face as Cole grabbed his phone off his belt holder and jumped up.

"Is there something you want to tell me?" Reed asked, first looking at Cole then back at Mitch.

"A van with the same logo was spotted near Bodig's house the night she was murdered."

Reed smiled. "So we do have a connection here."

The last thing Mitch would do was let the FBI take over when he needed to find Kat and make sure she was okay.

"Possibly." Mitch stood. "We'll look into it and get back to you."

"Now wait a minute, Elliot. We need to partner on this."

"Agreed. If you'll give me your card, I'll speak to my supervisor in the morning and get back to you."

Reed wasn't pleased, but he gave Mitch his card anyway. "See that you do get back to me." His tone was mildly threatening, but Mitch didn't care. He only wanted to get rid of the guy so he could check on Kat.

"Now if you'll excuse us." Mitch gestured toward the door and waited for Reed to march off before joining Cole who was still on the phone. His head was bent and he massaged the back of his neck.

Mitch felt his anxiety heighten at what didn't look like good news. "What's happening?"

Cole looked up. "Kat isn't answering her phone. I also sent her a 911 text. No reply."

"Maybe her battery died," Mitch offered.

"We're getting a GPS signal, so she still has battery."

"We?"

"Dani's at the office tracking the GPS on her computer."

Cole's attention turned to his phone, his gaze going to the ceiling. He listened then his eyes flew to Mitch. "Any idea why Kat would be in Newberg?"

Newberg? "My sister's in rehab in Newberg."

"I'm putting you on speaker, Dani." Cole thumbed his phone then held it out. "Dani, if Mitch gives you the rehab's address, can you confirm if Kat's GPS matches that location?"

"Of course." Dani's concerned voice came over the speaker.

Mitch scrolled through his contacts until he found the rehab facility then rattled off the address.

"Good," Dani said, and then he heard clicking. "Kat's not at the facility."

"So they're not together?" Mitch shared a worried look with Cole. "Unless Angie bailed. Let me call the clinic to see what's going on."

"While you do that I'll check Kat's recent call log to see who she talked to last," Dani offered.

Mitch went to his contacts again. Man, he was thankful for the advent of smart phones. The variety of apps gave them plenty of opportunity to get a lead on Kat's location. He dialed the rehab center and when someone answered, he explained his situation and was put on hold.

Cole started pacing, and Mitch settled for tapping his foot against the floor as fear continued to gnaw at his gut. If Kat were with him, she'd tell him not to worry, but to pray. Especially now that she was trying not to worry and trust God more. She was still struggling with it, but he'd seen her find some peace as she let it go. Maybe he could do the same thing.

"I'm sorry, Mr. Elliot," the woman finally said. "But your sister has checked herself out."

"When?"

"This afternoon."

"Thank you." He ended the call. "Angie's AWOL."

"She may be gone, but Kat talked to someone at the

rehab place around three," Dani said, still obviously concerned. "Does Angie have a cell or would she use the facility's phone?"

"She doesn't have a cell." Mitch took a few deep breaths. "Okay, so maybe we're overreacting here. Looks like Angie bailed, but before she did, she called Kat. She knew I wouldn't come get her, so she probably asked Kat for a ride back to the city."

One of their young clerks came into the room and held out a folder. "DNA for your case, Detective."

Mitch snatched the file from her hands, and she looked at him as if he'd lost his mind before she made an about-face. Mitch ran a finger down the page. "Granby's DNA didn't match the scrapings from Kat's fingernails and there's no other match in the system."

"So Granby isn't our guy and the man who attacked her is still out there." Cole's tone was dire. "We need to get out of here and find Kat now."

"Agreed," Mitch said, tossing the file on his desk. "We can use the GPS coordinates."

"She's on the move," Dani said. "So you'll need to stay in touch with me."

Mitch didn't waste a second but ran for the elevator with Cole's heavy shoes thumping right behind.

"Construction vans sometimes have GPS locators on them," Cole said while they waited for the elevator car. "Dani, we now know that the van we've been tracking belongs to Norton Construction. Do your thing to locate it and see if they have GPS installed."

"What thing?" Mitch asked.

"Dani's a computer expert. If that van has GPS, she'll find it."

The elevator dinged, and they boarded the car. As the doors slid closed, Mitch felt as if the walls were closing in on him.

He'd felt this inept and ineffective only once before. When Lori lost her life in front of him.

He clenched his jaw, his teeth grinding over the irony of the situation. He'd transferred his fear from losing Lori to Kat. That was the reason he wasn't with her right now and because of that a killer could be coming after not only the woman he loved, but his sister, as well.

SEVENTEEN

"I'm gonna throw up," Angie said and clutched her stomach.

Kat eased the car onto the shoulder and waited while Angie flung open the door and worked through a bout of dry heaves then lay back limp in the passenger seat.

"You're sure you want to do this?" Kat smiled at Angie, who was now shivering.

"Yes." Angie pulled her jacket tighter. "I don't need rehab to get straight."

Kat grabbed a blanket from her backseat. She settled it around Angie and brushed her hair back from her face. The face that looked so much like Mitch's. Guilt took over for a moment and Kat considered calling him. After Angie phoned for a ride, Kat had silenced her cell. She was afraid the rehab staff would call him and Kat knew he'd be mad if he found out she was helping Angie. Kat hadn't intended to help her leave, but to talk her into staying.

Angie looked up at her, her lips pressed into flat lines. "You're a good person, Kat, and I'm sorry I got you involved in my mess."

"I'm happy to help."

"You really mean that, don't you?"

"Why wouldn't I?"

She shot out her arm with angry red needle marks dotting

the inside. "When good people like you see this they usually run the other way."

"You have a problem, Angie, but that doesn't mean you're not a good person, too." Kat took Angie's hand. "Do you mind if I pray for you?"

"Not that it'll work, but okay."

Kat closed her eyes and held tight to Angie's trembling hand as she asked God to give her the strength and courage to give up drugs. To return to rehab if that was what she should do.

Kat opened her eyes. Angie was eyeing her. "Didn't seem to help."

"Prayer isn't an instant fix. Especially if you don't want to change." Kat searched Angie's troubled eyes. "Do you really want to change?"

She shrugged. "Let's just get going, okay?"

She cared too much about Mitch just to let this conversation drop. "Mitch loves you and misses you, Angie."

"That why he left me in jail the other night?"

"He explained that to you. Remember?"

"I remember what he said, but I know he's just embarrassed to be my brother and wanted to make me do what he wants me to do."

Kat shook her head. "That's the withdrawal talking. Mitch does everything because he loves you. Pure and simple, he loves you and wants to help you."

"How do you know?"

"Trust me. I know what a person who just wants to get his way is like and that's not your brother."

Angie simply stared at Kat. She wasn't getting through to her. Kat needed to tell Angie about her birth father so she could see that Mitch acted out of love. "My dad was exactly the way you're describing Mitch. Dad always thought he knew what was best for us and forced us to do what he wanted. My mom couldn't do anything without his permission. If he even suspected she went against him, he'd beat her."

Sorrow from the memories had Kat shaking her head and breathing deeply before going on. "But on my eleventh birthday, she decided to ignore his wishes and take me to the movies. She waited for him to go to work on the night shift and then she told me we were going. I was so excited. I'd never been anywhere fun and especially not somewhere with just my mom. But Dad forgot his supper on the counter and came back. He caught us walking to the bus stop, and he dragged her by her hair into the house. He ended up killing her, Angie. Right there in front of me."

Angie's eyes had opened wide. "Mitch would never do something like that."

"I know he wouldn't." Kat squeezed Angie's hand. "He's a good man, and he wants you to go to rehab because he loves you."

She smiled for the first time. "Because he loves me."

"So, do you still want to take off or go back to rehab?"

"Do you really think I can do this?"

"I know you can." Kat gave another squeeze.

"Okay." She nodded, a spark of resolve now in her eyes so like Mitch's. "I'll give it another try."

"Good." Kat settled behind the steering wheel and started the car. She eased onto the highway and the second she found a place to turn around, she did. She couldn't wait to get Angie settled and tell Mitch about the breakthrough.

But there wouldn't be any telling, would there?

Her joy faded to sadness. He'd made it clear that he didn't want a future with her when he'd shut her out that night. And in two days, he hadn't attempted to talk to her at all. He might never try to again. She was willing to open her heart and consider a future with him, but he was the one who had to let go of his fears for that to happen. And she just couldn't see him doing that in the near future.

Mitch had the lights and siren running, and he still couldn't move as fast as he wanted through traffic. Cole tried to arrange for a chopper, but in the end, it would take longer for a chopper to arrive and for them to get to a heliport than for them to just drive to Kat's location.

Cole sat in the passenger seat holding his cell phone. Derrick had taken over the call so Dani—who had indeed done her thing and located the van information—could determine if the vehicle had GPS. Every now and then, they could hear her mumble something that sounded like she was striking out.

"I've got it." Mitch heard Dani screaming in the background. "Tell them the van has GPS, and I'm almost there."

"She has—" Derrick started.

"We heard her," Cole said, interrupting his brother.

"Any change in Kat's location?" Mitch asked.

"She's headed in the same direction since she made that U-turn," Derrick answered. "If you both keep up the same speed you should meet her in about ten minutes."

"Oh, my gosh! No! Oh, no," Dani shouted, and Mitch's heart started thumping harder.

"What is it?" Cole asked.

"The van," Dani cried. "I have the GPS. It has almost identical coordinates to Kat. He's right behind her."

As the miles flew by, a light in the rearview mirror caught Kat's eye. They'd been alone on the road for the entire trip so it caught her by surprise. The vehicle seemed to be coming at a good clip, shooting a bolt of adrenaline into her heart.

Relax, Kat. Granby is behind bars. You're just being paranoid.

She took a few deep breaths and glanced at Angie to be

sure she wore her seat belt. She was softly snoring, the belt rising and falling with her breaths. Good. She was buckled. And it was good that she was sleeping; she needed the rest.

Kat checked the mirror again. The vehicle kept coming closer. Was probably planning to pass her. She reached for her phone.

"Just in case," she whispered to herself.

She glanced in the mirror again, and her heart iced over. The type of vehicle was clear now. A full-size van. Still didn't mean it was coming after them, though.

Kat kept her eyes on the road and unlocked her phone. The screen came to life and she noticed a bunch of missed calls. Mitch had likely figured out she and Angie were together.

The van was speeding up. Pressing forward. Moving closer. She saw the color. White. She rested her thumb over 9 and checked the mirror again. A black circle logo.

"Oh, no," she said and pressed the 9, then the 1.

The van surged faster than she expected and rammed them hard. Her phone flew from her hand as the tires slipped off the pavement. She grabbed the steering wheel and jerked to the left. The car careened across the road, hitting the shoulder on the other side. She jerked the other way. The van hit them again, but didn't back off. Crashing, shrieking, grinding metal split the quiet.

Angie woke up.

Please, God. Please don't let anything happen to Angie. Mitch would never survive another loss.

The wheel wrenched out of Kat's hand and she couldn't keep them on the road. "Brace yourself, Angie," she screamed as the front half of the car left the pavement.

They hit a rut and the car became airborne.

I'm sorry, Mitch was all she could think as they catapulted end over and end. Her world turned upside down in a blur of tall grasses and tree branches that threatened to fade to black.

* * *

"Both vehicles stopped moving," Dani announced.

"How far ahead?" Mitch asked, straining to see down the road.

"About two miles."

"Let's not give Norton advance notice of our arrival." Mitch flipped off the siren and light bar.

As they climbed to the top of the last hill separating them from Kat, he turned off his headlights and slowed to a crawl.

"There," Cole announced. "At the bottom of the hill. The van."

Mitch came to a stop when he caught sight of the vehicle. The driver's door was flung open. The front end was seriously damaged and there was no sign of Kat's car. GPS said her cell phone was here and that could only mean in the ravine. His heart took a dip and felt as if it might not come back.

"He's run her off the road, and he's checking to make sure he's killed her. Only one door open, so looks like there's only one guy," Mitch finally said and looked at Cole for a long moment.

"Then we have good odds." Cole's eyes reflected the seriousness of the night. "We need to get down there, but he can't know we're here."

"We can coast a little closer then we'll have to hoof it." Mitch cut the engine and put the car in Neutral. They rolled down the hill, picking up speed until he steered onto the shoulder, still out of view from the van.

"Let's go," Mitch said, and they slipped from the car. He grabbed his vest from the trunk and tossed it at Cole.

"No, you take it," Cole said, but Mitch took off before he could give it back.

Mitch heard the vest's tabs rip open behind him, certain he'd done the right thing. He could never bear to look at Kat again if her brother had been killed. As he drew his weapon, he only hoped he had the chance to look into those amazing brown eyes again.

They closed in on the van, and he spotted an area where the scrub had been flattened by tires. Just the thought of what Norton might've done to Kat sent Mitch's anger burning bright, and he couldn't wait to get his hands on Norton.

At the front of the van, he and Cole split up, one taking the front the other the back to clear the vehicle. Once they confirmed it was empty, he hurried into the ditch and heard Cole doing the same thing near the rear of the van. Mitch climbed over fallen pines and through waist-high grass, following the path where the tall brush had been flattened.

No sign of Norton, but Mitch did find Kat's car resting on the roof at the bottom of the incline.

God, no. Not like Lori. Not again. Please, not again.

He wanted to run, but he had to move slowly and watch for Norton. He crouched low and, keeping his weapon extended, eased closer. The vehicle had rolled several times and the top was seriously dented. Holding his breath, he approached the driver's side.

"Kat," he whispered and looked in, fear over finding her sending his heart into a fast rhythm.

She wasn't there, but Angie was strapped upside down in the passenger's side. He circled the back of the vehicle.

"Angie," he whispered.

"Mitchy," she answered, and his heart soared. "I'm sorry, Mitchy." She started crying. "I'm sorry. It's my fault Kat came out here, and I don't know what happened to her."

"Shh," he said, and leaned inside the vehicle to assess the situation. "The man who ran you off the road is out here somewhere. You have to talk quieter, okay?"

She nodded and sobbed quietly.

Amazingly, there was no major bleeding. "I can't risk moving you in case you have serious injuries that I can't see."

"I'm okay here. Go find Kat."

"Any idea where she is?"

"I don't know. I think I passed out. When I woke up, she was gone. Maybe she went for help."

"She wouldn't leave you alone. Not my Kat." His words rang out and he chastised himself for forgetting to keep his voice down.

"Then find her, Mitchy. This guy is after her, not me. I'll be fine."

He didn't want to leave his sister, but if Kat wasn't by Angie's side, she had to be in trouble. He couldn't protect them both. Angie was in the least amount of danger right now, as far as he could tell. If she passed out, she could have a concussion or worse. But he had to go. Had to find Kat. He needed help.

God, if You're there, I need Your help. Please. I can't save them both. I have to trust Angie to You. Don't take her from me, Lord. Protect her. Keep her safe. And let me find Kat.

He waited for that amazing peace he'd once felt when he used to trust God, but he only felt a sense of certainty in what he had to do. Find Kat.

"I love you, bug," he whispered.

"Me, too."

"Kat's brother Cole is here, too. You can trust him." Heart aching, he kissed her cheek and backed out of the vehicle.

If Kat had been in the car when Norton got down here, she'd be dead and so would Angie. So she must have climbed out to help Angie, and Norton had grabbed her then. The thought of that man putting his hands on her sent him into a blind rage, but he fought it off before he did something dumb and cost Kat her life.

He navigated the brush circling the car. The grass had

been trampled as if Kat had come around the front of the vehicle. Then it flattened out in a large pattern. Maybe from a struggle. Just what he feared. Norton had her, and it was up to him to track them down and save her life.

EIGHTEEN

The man clamped his arm around Kat's ribs, bruising flesh already tender from the seat belt. His other hand was pressed against her mouth and she struggled to breathe as he dragged her deeper into the woods. She recognized his cologne and his voice, sending shivers of fear over her body. He was the man who'd tried to kill her at Nancy's house. Now he was doing a great job of knocking her injured leg into rocks and trees, letting pain slice up her leg.

She managed to open her mouth and bite him.

"You little witch," he hissed and jerked his hand free.

"Stop," she cried out. "My leg is broken."

He didn't stop, but hauled her up higher. Her foot hung limply below the break and black stars danced in front of her eyes.

"Please stop. It hurts."

"Tough." He clamped his palm over her mouth, this time tight as a vise, and kept going into thicker vegetation. Pain washed over her, stole her breath and made her weak. He slowed and dumped her in the tall grass sending nausea rolling in her stomach and sweat breaking out over her face.

He squatted next to her, his gun trained on her heart. "If you try to signal him, he's dead, too. You got that?"

Kat knew he meant Mitch. They'd seen him talking to

Angie, though they hadn't been able to hear the entire conversation when this guy had decided they needed to move. Now he wanted to kill Mitch to keep him from arresting him. One shot and he'd take Mitch out. She wouldn't let that happen.

Fear strangled her breath, but she forced it away and sat up. Dizziness swirled, and she shook it off. If she was going to figure out how to get away from him without anyone getting hurt, she had to distract him by talking to him. "Who are you?"

"Like you don't know."

"If I knew I wouldn't ask."

He didn't take his focus from where they'd last seen Mitch. "Nice try. But I'll never buy your lie. Nancy Bodig said she showed the company books to you."

"What? What books? I don't know anything about any books."

"Then why did she hire you?"

"To find you—the man who killed her brother," Kat said, hazarding a guess.

"I didn't even know she had a brother. Whoever killed him it wasn't me."

"So why did you kill her, then?"

He quickly glanced at her, but even after he looked away, his penetrating gaze stayed with her. "She was my accountant, and she took the wrong set of books home. I couldn't risk her turning me in for money laundering. When she said she'd hired a P.I. to investigate, you had to go, too."

"Of all the stupid mistakes." She let disgust fill her voice. "She thought you were following her because of her brother. I doubt she even looked at the books."

His mouth dropped open.

She needed to take advantage of his stunned state. She lunged to her feet, but when she put pressure on her injured leg, she crumpled to the ground.

"Don't be stupid," he hissed, then jabbed his gun into her temple.

"Killing me will just make things worse for you," she said. "I used to be a cop, and cops take care of their own. They'll hunt you down with a vengeance."

"Shut up." He glared at her, but she had to go on.

"Mitch's a cop, too. Taking him out guarantees you'll be caught."

"I said, shut up!" he shouted, and Kat hoped Mitch heard him. He jabbed the gun harder, the cold metal bit like a snake. "You're just begging me to take you out."

"You can kill me, but you'll never get away. If Mitch is here that means other cops are on the way."

"Just be quiet and give me some time to think." He smacked her across the face with his gun.

The impact jerked her to the side. Blackness clouded her vision, and she stilled to stem off the darkness that came with the smallest of movements. There was no way she could fight this man off by herself. Mitch was her only hope. But where was he?

She listened to the sounds of the night. Crickets chirped and wind gently rustled the grass and trees, but other than that…silence. Still, she knew Mitch was here. She'd seen him taking care of his sister and trying to calm her. She also heard him say she was *his Kat*. *His Kat* as if she belonged to him and he was looking for her.

She closed her eyes and reminded herself that God was here with her.

I'll give up my life for him, Father. Please don't let his search for me lead him to his death.

Mitch was almost there. He could see Kat lying on the ground and Norton squatting next to her, his weapon aimed at her. Problem was Mitch didn't have a plan to rescue her.

He couldn't rush the guy or he'd plug him with a bullet or worse yet, turn and fire on Kat.

He could work his way around behind them but there was no way he could jump Norton before he took Kat out.

Mitch heard the barest hint of a rustle behind him.

Had to be Cole.

Mitch turned, his weapon at the ready, but as Cole stepped into view, Mitch lowered it and waited for Cole to join him.

Staying low, Cole crept closer seeming as if he melded with the brush. "What's going on?"

"Norton has Kat over there." He pointed to their location. "She's injured. Not sure how, but I heard her cry out in pain."

Cole hissed out a breath. "Norton the only one?"

"As far as I can tell."

"Then we can take him. One of us needs to act as a decoy to draw his fire. The other can circle around and attack him from the rear."

This sounded like the best option, but Mitch wouldn't let Kat's brother be the decoy. "I'll stay here and draw his fire."

"No. I'm the decoy."

"I can't let you do that."

He studied Mitch for a long moment. "I'm the one wearing the bulletproof vest. Besides, I twisted my ankle back there, so it's better for me to stay put."

Mitch hadn't seen Cole limp, but he couldn't argue with the guy without drawing attention. "Should take me just a few minutes to get around them." He peered at Cole. "Don't try to be a hero and do something stupid."

Cole gave a clipped nod.

"I mean it, Cole," Mitch added. "I love your sister, and you better not make me tell her I got you killed."

"'Bout time you admitted how you felt about her." Cole smiled and flicked his hand to tell Mitch to take off.

He did, carefully placing one foot in front of the other to

keep his footfalls silent. He kept moving until he was close enough to hear Kat's ragged breathing. Likely from the pain.

"You can still take off. It's not too late," she said to Norton, but her words lacked conviction.

"You said yourself other cops are on the way and you're going to be my ticket out of here. So get up. I'm not going alone."

"My leg is broken."

"Either you stand up or I start firing in the direction of that cop you seem so fixed on protecting."

So she knew he was here. She must have been close by when he'd talked to Angie.

"Fine. I'll get up, just don't shoot at him." Injured and held captive, she was still trying to protect him.

His heart soared then fell. He should be the one doing the protecting. Caring for her. Helping her. Loving her. And he'd failed. Just like he'd failed Lori and once again, there was nothing he could do.

Lord, I need Your help. I get that I can't control everything and can't be everywhere at one time. But You can and I need You to be here now. With Kat. With Cole. With me. Help me... no us, to end this without anyone getting hurt.

"C'mon out, Norton," Cole yelled out. Mitch heard brush rustle and knew Cole was on the move to draw Norton's attention and his fire.

Norton's gun exploded, the flash blinding in intensity. *Pop, pop, pop.*

With a roar, Mitch leaped from his spot and tackled Norton from behind. He rolled, taking Mitch with him. Mitch knocked the weapon out of Norton's hand. He heard Kat fumbling for it. He broke free for a second, slammed his fist into Norton's face, and heard a satisfying crunch of bones. Norton retaliated with a punch of his own.

"Freeze!" Kat screamed. "Or I'll shoot."

Norton went still. Mitch grabbed his cuffs and slapped them on Norton's wrists, jerking them a little tighter than necessary.

"Cole. We have him. He's cuffed," Mitch yelled as he dug his flashlight from his pocket and aimed it at Kat. Mitch held his breath while running his light over her body. He noted a bloody pant leg and waited for a response from Cole. Nothing.

"Are you okay?" he asked, hating the terrified look on her face.

"I'm fine. Please go check on Cole. Hurry." Her frantic tone nearly had him bolting away, but he wasn't willing to risk leaving Norton anywhere near her even if he was cuffed, so Mitch jerked him to his feet. He shoved him onto beaten-down grass and shone his flashlight in front of Norton's feet.

"Cole?" Mitch called out. Nothing. He headed to the last location where he'd seen movement. The location Norton had fired those rounds into. He heard a moan ahead and moved faster.

Mitch found Cole lying on his side, his face pale and his hands clutching his chest. "Cole."

"See you got him," Cole said breathlessly. "Kat okay?"

"Her leg's broken, but otherwise I think she's fine. Where are you hit?"

"He plugged me dead center of my vest." Cole ripped the vest free and gulped deep breaths. He trained a harsh look on Norton, and Mitch pitied the person who ever crossed Cole Justice or hurt his family.

Sirens split the quiet, easing Mitch's concern for Kat and his sister a bit. "You called in reinforcements I see."

"Hey, I was once a marshal. You don't think I'd count on a cop for my only backup do you?" Cole laughed, then started coughing.

Mitch smiled. "If you're up to keeping this creep here, I'll go get Kat then we can check on my sister."

"Angie's a real spitfire. Made me come after you."

"That she is." Mitch forced Norton to sit with his back to a tree as Cole got up and stretched.

"What're you waiting for?" Cole barked. "Go rescue your damsel in distress."

With one last look to make sure Cole was fit to handle Norton, Mitch bolted toward Kat. He could finally tell her how much she'd come to mean to him, and God willing, Mitch hoped she wasn't too mad at him for running from her the other night to listen.

Kat lay on her back, fighting the pain and listening to the rustle of people moving about and the stilling of sirens as they reached them. She'd told Mitch she was fine, but her stomach was tight with worry.

What if Cole was hurt? Maybe dead? Any one of them could've died tonight.

She heard footfalls pounding her way and watched as Mitch burst through the thick brush. He smiled at her, his crooked grin tipping up at the corner, and she knew everything was okay.

"Cole's vest did its job," he said and dropped to his knees by her side. "He'll have a bruise, but he's fine."

"Thank You, God."

"Amen to that." He helped her sit up and held her shoulders. "How about I carry you out of here?"

She smiled up at him. "There is nothing I'd like more than to be held by you, but I think my leg needs a splint before I can move again. I'd better wait here for the paramedics."

He settled closer, bending low so he was nearly eye level with her and those eyes often as sharp as steel were soft and tender. He brushed wayward strands of hair from her face then slipped his arms around her back.

She smiled at his gentle touch, and moved toward him as

he lowered his head and kissed her. Softly, gently. Perfectly. She wrapped her arms around his neck and kissed him until she heard footfalls coming their way.

She eased back, and he took her hands in his. "So you want me to hold you, do you?"

She smiled again and seeing his eyes heat up in response she decided to throw caution to the wind and tell him exactly how she felt. "And never let go."

"Are you saying what I think you're saying?"

"I love you, Mitch," she said shyly.

"I love you, too, Kat Justice. Don't ever scare me like this again."

"It's not in my plans." She brushed her fingers down the side of his face, and he shivered. She loved seeing his reaction and knowing that he cared about her. Now she could only hope he'd decided to let go of his past and let her in.

"So," he said casually though she could see his pulse pounding at the base of his neck. "Once the doc patches you up again, how about we go on a date? You know something romantic with candles, and music."

Her smile faded. "You think you're ready for that? I mean with what happened to Lori and all?"

He stared into her eyes, and she held her breath as she waited for his answer.

"Being with you is all that matters." He cupped the side of her face, his fingers gentle. "Almost losing you made me see I'm willing to risk everything for you, Kat. Everything."

Risk everything? As in his life? She frowned.

"What?" he asked, his voice filled with dread. "What did I say?"

She shook her head. "When you said risk everything, my mind went to you being a cop and the risks you take."

"And you could never be with a cop, right?"

"No, I can," she said emphatically to counteract the insecurity in his voice. "I just need to remember to let God be in charge instead of worrying." She took a deep breath. "I'm not sure if I'll be able to let it go completely, but you are so worth trying for."

"We can work on that together."

She rested her forehead against his chest and knew he was right. They had things to overcome, but together they could do anything.

EPILOGUE

Mitch pulled to the curb in front of Kat's renovated house. It had taken another six months to finish the renovations but seeing the results was well worth the wait. The only clues that the place had suffered such severe damage last year were immature little plants surrounding the structure, contrasting with the older neighborhood's mature landscaping.

"I don't think I should be here, Mitch." Angie swiveled to face him and he was once again amazed at the transformation in her physical appearance. She'd kicked the drugs and was living with him. Eating regularly had filled out her face and she once again looked like a twenty-nine-year-old woman.

He took her hand and squeezed. "Of course you should."

"But look at this neighborhood. It's filled with classy people who won't want a drug addict around."

"A reformed addict is a whole different story, bug." He met her gaze and made sure she knew how proud he was of her transformation. "Besides you don't know what goes on behind all these closed doors. Probably a few prescription drug addicts on this street alone."

"But not in the Justice family."

"You're right. They're all clean and sober. But they won't look down on you. Each one of them has a past filled with things that keep them from judging others."

"You're sure?"

"I'm positive." He nodded and smiled at the thought of the amazing family waiting inside. The family who for the most part had opened their arms to include both him and Angie. "So, are you game?"

"Fine."

"That's my girl," he said and tweaked her nose. He grabbed his jacket and as he slipped into it, he felt the pocket to make sure the box holding his mother's ring sat where he'd stowed it before leaving home today. Lori had liked everything new so he'd bought a new engagement ring for her. But his mother's ring reminded him of the precious gift of family, and he knew it would be perfect for Kat.

When everyone went home tonight, he planned to ask her to marry him. Talk about something scary enough to make him not want to go inside, but he did and was soon surrounded by the Justices minus Kat.

Mitch introduced Angie to Ethan and his wife, Jennie. They engaged in small talk while Mitch searched the room for Kat. He didn't see her in the small groups of people chatting and laughing in the family room painted in a vivid blue just like Kat's personality.

"She's in the kitchen," Ethan said, looking at him with an appraising eye. The eldest of the Justices hadn't warmed up to Mitch. It was clear he didn't think Mitch was good enough for his sister. But Dani had told Mitch that Ethan would feel this way about any man who might seriously pursue Kat, to be patient and let Ethan get to know him.

Still, Mitch felt uneasy. He could hunt down and bring in a killer, but he withered under Ethan's intense scrutiny. He felt like the room temperature was rising with each second so he slipped off his jacket and draped it over his arm.

"I'll put that in the bedroom for you," Dani said, trying to take it from him.

He didn't want to part with the ring so he held firm, but when she eyed him up he released his hold, and she lost her balance. Derrick caught her, but she dropped the jacket and the ring box came tumbling out.

Dani gasped and clapped as her face brightened with excitement.

Ethan dropped down to get the black velvet box and rose with a scowl on his face.

"I was hoping to get a minute alone with all of you today." Mitch took back the ring. "I plan to propose to Kat tonight, and I was hoping for your blessing before I do."

Angie must have sensed his discomfort as she slipped her hand into his and gave it a squeeze much as he'd done with her in the car a few moments ago.

"You've got mine, Mitch." Dani gave him a quick hug before stepping back. "I'm sure the others feel the same way." She nudged Derrick.

"Ah, yeah, man," Derrick said and shook Mitch's hand. "I'm cool with it."

Cole stuck out his hand. "Welcome to the family."

"Well, she has to say yes before I'm part of the family." Mitch ended with a nervous laugh.

"She'll say yes." Cole stepped back and Mitch could tell this usually reserved guy was happy for them.

"Hurt her and you'll answer to all of us," Ethan grumbled, but he shook hands, too.

"Ignore the grump," Jennie said and gave Mitch a little hug. "He'll never think anyone's good enough for Kat, but we all know you'll make her happy."

"Then I guess all that's left is to ask Kat." He couldn't believe how nervous he was.

"Ask me what?" Kat's voice came from behind.

He palmed the ring while turning to look at the woman he hoped to spend the rest of his life with. She wore a simple white sundress and had her hair pulled back with soft tendrils just caressing the side of her face. He imagined his fingers touching the same spot, and he forgot about everyone else standing there. All he could think about as he walked toward her was taking that clasp out and running his fingers through hair he knew was soft and silky.

He took her hand and urged her out onto a deck overlooking lush green grass and surrounded by towering pine trees. He turned and saw everyone watching them through the French doors so he pulled her to the side and smiled down on her.

"What's going on?" she asked. This time her tone held worry.

He let go of her hand and got down on his knee. Her gasp of surprise gave him a moment's pause. Was it a good gasp or bad one? He had a whole speech planned, but when he looked up and saw love reflected in her eyes, he knew she'd say yes, and he didn't need a formal speech.

"I love you, Katherine Marie Justice. More than I ever thought was possible to love someone." He pulled out the ring box and opened the lid. "Will you marry me?"

"Yes," she whispered as tears slid down her cheeks.

He stood and put the ring on her finger. "This was my mother's ring."

She studied it. "It's perfect, Mitch. So perfect. It's almost like we get to share this day with your parents." She twined her arms around his neck and looked up, love for him burning in her eyes.

He lowered his head and claimed her lips as he heard a round of applause behind them. Reluctantly he lifted his head and was reminded of their first kiss when Kat had told Cole to get lost.

"You do know marrying me comes with all of them." She tipped her head at her family standing in the doorway. Dani had her arm around Angie and his sister glowed with a happiness he hadn't seen since their father died.

He smiled down on Kat. "I wouldn't have it any other way."

Today was a new beginning for both of them. He'd thought God didn't have his best interest at heart, but now, as he bent to kiss Kat again, he knew without a doubt he'd been wrong. Dead wrong.

* * * * *

Dear Reader,

Thank you for reading Kat and Mitch's story. I really felt convicted as I wrote their story centered around worry. Why? Because I was doing a lot of worrying before I started the book. One of the things Kat thinks early on in the book really encompassed my thoughts at the time.

Here it is: *She trusted God, she just wanted to help Him to make sure things didn't go wrong.*

Do you ever do that? Think you're trusting God no matter the outcome, but then find yourself doing little things to help Him along when things don't seem to be going your way? I did before writing *Dead Wrong*. But now, I'm trying to let go and let God. It's not always easy, but when worry pops up now, I remember Kat and Mitch's struggles and I'm able to let go much more easily. It's my prayer that when worry assails you, you, too, can give it up and rest in God's peace.

I love to hear from readers and you can reach me through my website, www.susansleeman.com, or in care of Love Inspired Books at 233 Broadway, Suite 1001, New York, NY 10279.

Susan Sleeman

Questions for Discussion

1. Kat and Mitch both worry. Not about the little things of life, but about the big life-or-death matters. Do you worry, and if so about what?

2. Has worrying ever accomplished anything good in your life or do you wish you could let it go? After reading the book are there ways that you can let go of that worry?

3. Why do you think it took Kat so long to see how much she worried?

4. Kat discovers that worrying is second-guessing God and is sinful. Have you really thought about worry as being sinful before? Do you trust God with everything or are there certain things that you hold on tightly to? If so, what are they?

5. After losing the woman he loved, Mitch is terrified of loving again. Have you ever felt this way after a relationship ended and if so, how did you work through it?

6. Kat's father was an abusive, controlling man and Kat can't handle someone trying to control her in any way. How about you? How do you feel when someone wants to control what you do?

7. When Mitch's sister comes to him for help after repeatedly hurting him with her drug use, he gives in and lets her stay at his home for the night. What would you have done in this situation?

8. When Mitch's sister finally gets clean, she thinks she isn't good enough for other people. Is there something you're harboring in your heart that makes you think less of yourself?

9. Mitch goes behind Kat's back and involves her family in a dangerous situation. Do you think what he did was justified, or should he have talked to her first?

10. When life got too difficult, Mitch turned away from God. We all turn away in degrees, maybe not rejecting God as Mitch did, but rejecting some of the things He would have us do in our lives. Have you ever had anything in your life that made you turn away? How did you come back from it?

11. Which character in the story do you relate most to and why?

12. In my letter, I shared a section of the book that really spoke to some issues I was facing when I wrote it. Is there a particular scene in the book that you can relate to?

13. After writing the first two books in The Justice Agency series, I have really come to like Cole's no-nonsense approach to life and am now really enjoying writing his story. Do you know anyone like Cole, who can cut away all the fluff and get to the heart of a problem? Or are you a person like that and if so, how did you come to be that way?